I0657608

REQUIEM FOR TITUS

REQUIEM FOR TITUS
Published by
BIRDCALL PUBLISHING AUSTRALIA
www.brendacheersbooks.com
Copyright © 2016 Brenda Cheers
All rights reserved.
First Edition
Author image Sargaison / Brisbane Headshots
Cover images © IS_ImageSource / iStockphoto.com
© Tamara Dragovic / iStockphoto.com
© Armin Staudt / shutterstock.com
ISBN-13: 978-0-9942079-9-9 (Print)

All rights reserved.
First Edition
Author image Sargaison / Brisbane Headshots
Cover image © IS_ImageSource / iStockphoto.com
Interior Format & Design by Julieann Wallace
lillypillypublishing@outlook.com

This book is a work of fiction and any resemblance to persons, living or dead, or places, events or locales is purely coincidental. The characters are productions of the author's imagination and used fictitiously.

All Rights Reserved. No part of this publication may be reproduced, stored in, or introduced into a retrieval system, or transmitted, in any form, or by any means (electronic, mechanical, photocopying, recording or otherwise) without the prior written permission of the publisher.

ALSO BY BRENDA CHEERS

The Strange Worlds Series:
In Strange Worlds
In a Time Where They Belong
Cato's Prophecy

In Conversations with Strangers
The Secrets of Julia Hawke

REQUIEM FOR TITUS

Strange Worlds # 4

Brenda Cheers

Bravery is not a quality of the body.
It is of the soul.
—Mahatma Gandhi

PROLOGUE

My name is Melisandre and I have a story to tell. It is an important story that will answer questions asked by people in the centuries to come.

It is the year 2059 and I live in Maleny, Queensland, Australia. My grandparents on my mother's side are the original survivors of the 2013 pandemic, Luke and Connie. On my father's side, they are George and Heather.

I am twenty-three years old, but this story began when I was about to turn thirteen. That is when a series of events first began, and I think these caused changes in the future.

That's why I am writing this. Someone has to create a record of what occurred so that future generations will understand. I think this is important.

Grace thought it was, anyway. She instructed me to do this. She didn't trust Meg to record those events accurately in her diaries.

The only way to tell this story is from the beginning, on a cold morning in early July, a week before my thirteenth birthday.

IN THE FOREST

I woke early, my eyes flying open as soon as the birds began warming up their voices. There was a pinkish glow in the sky from the sun that was rising in the east.

Sliding out of bed gently, so as not to wake my little sisters who were snuggled in beside me, I felt for my overalls and thrust my legs into them. A pair of socks were under my pillow, where I'd left them the night before. That way they were easy to find in the semi-darkness, and also they were slightly warm. I slid them over my feet, in preparation for the cold floor.

Before I could leave our cabin, I had to negotiate my way around all the small figures lying in various positions on mattresses spread over the floor. These were my siblings who were jammed into whatever space was available. I knew that if any of my little brothers or sisters woke and saw me leaving, they would want to follow me.

I checked the big pocket at the front of my overalls to make sure my notebook was there. Once outside, I grabbed a coat from the row of hooks and then pushed my feet into rubber boots. Only then did I stop to admire the morning.

I can't tell you how wonderful it felt that day to be able to walk, unfettered, across the clearing to the forest which bordered the settlement. I heard the frosted grass crunching under my boots, felt the cold air filling my lungs.

I knew exactly where to go. There was a small cleared patch in the forest where there were two objects, a fallen log and a tree stump. I often went there to write, knowing I could perch on the log while resting the notebook on the stump. These were precious times, my snatches of peace and quiet. Rare and beautiful.

Within minutes I was immersed in my story. What I wrote back then were short tales for the younger children. Mostly they were about the terrible things that happened to boys and girls when they were naughty. My pencil flew across the page, trying to keep up with the ideas flowing from my imagination. The Boo-gang, which was a hulking, ugly, bear-like creature, was just about to swoop on two boys who had stolen a pie and run down the road to eat it. I was excited, wondering what was going to happen next.

Then I felt something that made me freeze. It was a hot breath on the back of my neck. The story I was writing was scary, so when I felt this, my first thoughts were that something evil was behind me. I didn't dare turn to look. I told myself that it might just be an untethered horse or other animal. I took a deep breath and swivelled around.

"Gareth! Don't sneak up on me like that!"

My friend's laugh was wicked. "Scared you, didn't I?"

"Yes you did, and that was mean. What are you doing here at this hour?"

"Came to see you. It's hard at other times. We don't get to hang out much."

This was true, but I didn't like to share my special magic time with anyone else. On the other hand, I didn't want to hurt Gareth's feelings. I smiled at him. "Yeah, I know what you mean. No spare time, hey? How did you know I'd be here?"

"I've seen you before, walking across the clearing. You know I don't sleep much…"

"Yeah, you've told me that."

"What's the story about?"

I told Gareth about the Boo-gang and saw him shiver.

"Creepy." Gareth stepped over the log and sat down next to me. He then shuffled along until our thighs were just about touching. I sensed something about him then—something I hadn't felt before. It was a change of mood, a surge of excitement. He shifted even closer until his leg was putting pressure on mine. I shifted away a little.

"So, what's new?" He asked this while trying to hold my gaze. I normally enjoyed looking into his eyes because they were so special. They were the sparkly blue/green/lilac eyes that only a few in the community had. That day, however, his gaze made me nervous. I looked away.

"Not much. You?"

He put a hand on my knee.

"I heard your mum talking to Heather the other day."

"Oh?"

"Said you'd started bleeding."

A blush crept up my neck and filled my face. "So?"

"So, you're a woman now." He shifted again so the gap I had created disappeared. The hand on my knee began moving higher up my leg. I slid away from him and snapped my notebook shut.

"I don't understand what business that is of yours. It's private. You shouldn't have been eavesdropping."

Gareth's face took on a contrite expression that I didn't trust. "Hey." He opened his arms. "Sorry. It's just that you'll need a boyfriend soon."

I blinked slowly. A boyfriend. He wanted to be my boyfriend? I felt confused. "No…I don't think—"

"Just give me a little kiss, hey?" Gareth pushed his face up against mine and grabbed my breast.

I was stunned, not knowing what to do. I didn't want to hurt my friend's feelings, but didn't like how he was making me feel. I needed to escape from him and think. I moved away and grabbed my notebook. "Um—I've got to go and wake the little ones now. Mum will wonder where I am. I'll see you later."

"Wait! You haven't given me an answer."

"You didn't ask me anything."

"Well, I said you'd need a boyfriend--"

I shoved the notebook back into the bib of my overalls. "Later," I said as I moved quickly back to the clearing. From there I ran as fast as my rubber boots would allow, back to the sanctuary of my family's cabin where I knew my brothers and sisters would soon be stirring.

Gareth inherited his special sparkly eyes because of a strange series of events. The old time traveller, William and our leader Meg once had a brief encounter which resulted in a child who Meg named Will.

There were twin girls in the community who both fancied Will, but he loved one and rejected the other. Leena, the rejected girl, managed to seduce Will just the once. The new super-fertility that had been present in the community since the pandemic resulted in two sets of twins being born to the sisters within days of each other. All four children had the special eyes. They were also intellectually gifted, having inherited the genes of, not only old William with his brain from the future, but also their grandmother, India, who was a geneticist.

Gareth, born to Leena, was one of these gifted children. The trouble was that his special talents seemed to be at odds with his personality. He had always been hyperactive, since birth I was told. He never slept well and couldn't sit still for long.

In the schoolhouse, Grandma Heather had set up a separate area in the front right corner for Will's children. The shelf next to their desks was crammed full of special text books and materials. Will would visit the schoolhouse several times a week to teach his children advanced mathematics, physics, and chemistry. It was during these lessons that Gareth always seemed to get into trouble. His restlessness and lack of concentration frustrated Will, who often sent his son elsewhere. When this happened, a resentful Gareth would run home to his mother.

Members of the community often spoke about Gareth's mother in hushed tones and I would creep closer to hear what they were saying. Usually there was talk about Leena's instability and irrational behaviour. She treated Gareth like a small child, even when he became a teenager. He adopted the habit of throwing tantrums, knowing Leena would give in to them. His twin sister, Isabella, was a good child who frowned at the antics of her brother.

I was flattered when Gareth first became friendly toward me. The sparkly-eyed kids always seemed to stick together. In class they acted as though they were far superior to the rest of us. To have one of them want to be my friend? Well, that was wonderful.

Deep down I knew there was something a bit different about Gareth, maybe a bit broken or something, but that was okay with me. I had a special, sparkly-eyed friend and I was happy. Until that morning in the forest.

A few weeks before Gareth became over-friendly, my mother had spoken to me about being a woman. She told me that I had to be careful. The increased fertility in our community meant that most pregnancies resulted in twins. She warned me about being alone with boys and explained what they would want to do with me.

"Make sure you're ready, Honey-bee," she said while brushing my hair. "It will happen eventually—you'll be a mother many times over—but pick a nice boy first."

I nodded. I certainly didn't feel ready yet.

"Once you start down this track," she continued, "you'll likely end up like me—the tired mother of brood of children." She sighed and looked around the cramped cabin. "Everyone will tell you that you must help re-populate the world. That's true, but it doesn't have to happen right away."

I hugged my mother then. It was the first time I realised she might not be happy with her life. She was considered a beautiful woman, with dark auburn hair and olive skin. She had almond-shaped eyes the colour of chocolate.

High cheekbones and a full mouth rounded off her perfect features. I reckoned she was the most beautiful woman in our settlement. My father adored her. I always thought she was contented and happy.

"You just have to be firm and say 'No!'" she said. "Don't let the boys manipulate you, not until you are completely ready to take this step. You're an attractive girl. There will be a lot of interest."

Attractive? I didn't think I was. I didn't have Mum's red hair. Mine was brown. I did have big eyes, but they weren't as pretty as Mum's. It was nice to hear Mum say I was attractive, though. She went on to say, "Look at my mother—how she has turned out. All those pregnancies..." Mum shook her head sadly.

Grandma Connie was only in her early fifties, but looked a great deal older. Her body was lumpy and shapeless, with legs and ankles that were always swollen. She rarely left her and Grandpa Luke's cabin anymore, even for special occasions. Every night, Grandpa Luke would sit with the elders in the community hall during dinner, but would take his and Connie's food back to their cabin so they could eat together. His devotion and loyalty to her was still as strong as when he'd first rescued her in 2013. I hardly knew Grandma Connie and couldn't remember ever having had a lengthy conversation with her.

"And," my mother continued, "if I'm not careful, I'll end up like her. All the women here are in danger of that."

Later, when I was outside and looking around the community, I saw that my mother's concerns were well-founded. Most of the daughters of the original survivors looked as though they'd had the life sucked out of them, while their daughters seemed headed for a similar fate. The men, on the other hand were still youthful and energetic.

I made the decision then that I wouldn't end up like the other women. I'd take my time and delay my first pregnancy for as long as possible. I would make sure my body had matured and strengthened first. The longer I delayed breeding, the fewer pregnancies I would have overall.

Then Gareth began trying to seduce me and I realised how hard this was going to be. I was just turning thirteen, for heaven's sakes. I'd have to be on my guard at all times. I felt the weight of this, became more aware of the looks that came from all the teenage boys. Sometimes in the schoolhouse when I was bending over a child, or picking something up off the floor, I'd feel someone pass behind me and often I felt a touch at the same time. It might be on the hip, or bottom, or leg. When I turned around, it would be to see one of the teenage boys grinning at me.

This problem weighed on my mind constantly. That was until other events overtook these worries and they faded into the background.

BIRTHDAY DINNER

The community dining hall was crowded and noisy. Food was being laid out on long tables, while small children ran around whooping at the top of their lungs. Adults tried to quieten them, but with little success. I sat still, not wanting to mess up my dress or hair, both of which I'd prepared with care. I tried to hide the excitement that quivered inside me.

Sunday night dinners were always special. George and his helpers would make exotic dishes. There would be music and entertainment. Sometimes there was even dancing. It was always wonderful.

Although our leader Meg lived apart from the rest of us, she had never been known to miss a Sunday night dinner.

She would enter the hall punctually, just as everybody took their seats. She would smile and nod to various people and inspect the food before being seated at the elders' table.

This particular night was special to me because it was my thirteenth birthday. Although there were a great many children and lots of birthdays, only the passing into teenage-hood was publicly celebrated. At thirteen a child earned the right to dine with adults during the week, and was given more responsibility on a daily basis. The Sunday night closest to this special birthday was when the celebration took place. My twin, Zac, and I were the two 'special guests' on this night. There would be cake.

The food was distributed down the long benches and everybody waited impatiently for the last person to be served so they could begin eating. That's when a murmur began echoing around the hall. Mum looked at Dad with a frown. "Meg hasn't arrived," she said. Other people began looking around and I could hear Meg's name over and over again. Will stood and went to the door. He came back, shrugging his shoulders. "Mum's just late. Get started everyone."

The food was wonderful and I ate quickly. Mum smiled at me, knowing I was excited about my cake. Time went by and I kept watching the door, hoping Meg would make it in time to see Zac and me blow out the candles.

But she didn't arrive. I heard Dad say to Mum that somebody should go and check on her. She was an old woman and anything could have happened.

George carried the cake out with pride. It was one of the best things I had seen in my whole life. It was tall and covered in cream and strawberries. The cake inside was vanilla, my favourite. Thirteen candles burned on the top.

Everybody sang happy birthday and I blew out the candles. These were re-lit so that my brother could have his turn at blowing them out. It felt hollow, though, without Meg there. I felt like crying.

Dad went to Will and volunteered to drive to Meg's house to see if she was alright. Will smiled and thanked him, but said to relax. If she hadn't shown up by the morning, he'd go and check on her. He was sure there was nothing wrong.

Mum gave me a rueful smile that said she understood my disappointment. In a community teeming with children, the chance to feel special was very rare.

Will didn't go to his mother's house early the next morning. He needed to set up some experiments in his workshop first. I was rostered to help him on that particular day—something I truly enjoyed—so I helped him with the necessary tasks.

Will liked me helping him, saying I was his favourite assistant. He liked the fact I didn't talk much and that I did what I was told without fuss. He never had to tell me what to do twice.

This caused problems between Will and my grandma Heather. My grandmother said I was needed in the schoolroom because I was great with the younger kids. She considered me to be her successor. Will said that his work was more important, as the survival of the human race depended on what he was working on and without my help, everything would take longer. Meg had to intervene and find a compromise. My time was divided between Heather and Will, formalised on a roster. I felt awkward about this and embarrassed by the attention.

During these negotiations between Will and Heather for my time, I noticed Meg looking at me with a frown that suggested she couldn't see what the fuss was about. Why were they fighting over me? In her eyes I wasn't anything special.

I liked being in both places, either place. I enjoyed teaching the younger children, but loved my time in Will's workshop. To be honest, I think I had a bit of a juvenile crush on Will, so that when he smiled and praised me, my heart beat so loudly that I feared he would hear it. My armpits would sweat, too, which I found weird.

Even though Will's oldest children were thirteen, he was still only thirty. He had black, thick hair that always flopped to his eyebrows and highlighted his sparkly eyes. His body, even under his lab coat, was extraordinary because of a fitness program he practised every day. What was there not to love about this gorgeous man? For a girl reaching puberty, he was dynamite.

On this morning, after my birthday dinner, Will and I set

up the experiments, which were all to do with sustainable sources of energy. When he was satisfied that everything was going to plan, Will removed his lab coat and handed it to me. "I'll take the Beast for a spin to Mum's." The Beast was an experimental vehicle that he'd been working on part-time for at least twelve months. It was powered by hydrogen cells and built from plans left behind by his father thirty years before. I waited until I heard the vehicle make its way down to the road and then grabbed a broom to sweep the floor.

Time moved slowly. I re-washed some beakers that still looked cloudy. I took everything off the main workbench and cleaned its surface. I washed the windows. Still Will didn't return. I sat on the floor and took the notebook from my pocket, but the pencil remained hovering over the page. The words wouldn't come.

Around lunchtime, I heard the Beast make its way up the driveway again. I leapt to my feet and ran to the window. Will was being mobbed by anxious people. His body language told me there was nothing wrong, that Meg was alright. He spoke to the group for a few minutes and then made his way back to the workshop. He was whistling.

I looked at Will in wonder. His face was different, somehow. He was wearing a smile that held secrets. His body seemed to be quivering with excitement, like a dog being teased with a big bone. I watched him check on the experiments and give satisfied grunts. He began making notes. Occasionally he would give a slight chuckle, which was out of character. I could tell that something was up, but knew he wasn't about to let me in on the secret.

But there were more strange happenings to come.

One day, Meg arrived and took India away.

This was the first anybody had seen of our leader for at least two weeks. She came up the driveway in her battered old four-wheel-drive and pulled up at the main house. She lowered herself to the ground slowly. She walked to the building that now housed India, a clinic of sorts, and closed the door. Grandfather George later told us that he could hear the two of them talking non-stop for a long time, but couldn't make out the words. Eventually, the door re-opened and Meg could be seen supporting India as they made painful progress to the vehicle. It took the two women some time to climb into the seats. They drove away without further comment.

I must tell you how sick India was. Breast cancer had invaded her body before she realised what was happening. Her lungs and bones were affected quickly. We all watched helplessly as this intelligent, hardworking woman became a dull-eyed skeleton who coughed constantly. It was clear she wouldn't see Christmas.

Now Meg had taken her away and we didn't know why. Had she decided to care for her friend? I saw people huddling in groups discussing this latest happening. Speculation was rife.

Nobody saw Meg or India for more than a week. On a warmer than average August day, there was a stir when Meg's vehicle was seen approaching. Everybody stopped working and watched as the car doors opened. India climbed down from the seat, unassisted. She was still very thin, but clearly in far better health. I watched Ruth run to her mother and grasp her shoulders. She looked into India's eyes and began crying, saying it was a miracle. Ruth turned to Meg for an explanation, but our leader was already climbing back into the car. She drove away quickly.

Will's other son, the one born to his wife Ruth, was named Jack. He was likeable enough—polite and friendly—but this was always tinged with a hint of superiority.

One day he decided to go fishing at Baroon Pocket Dam. Nobody had done this for a week or so, and the community needed some more supplies. He packed up some fishing rods and tackle and asked Will to drop him to the dam in the Beast. When Will collected his son several hours later, he found that the boy had caught a boatload of fish, enough to feed the whole community that evening. There was great celebration and Jack was made to feel like a hero.

I had been avoiding Gareth for the few weeks following his approach to me in the forest. I changed my mind, however, when I saw his reaction to Jack's success. Gareth's face was marred by a dark expression which I knew came from jealousy. I also knew that my friend was not good at handling this sort of emotion. I walked up behind him.

"Hey," I said.

Gareth was silent for a moment. Finally, I heard a 'hey' in response.

I put my hand on his shoulder. "I reckon the fish will taste like a dog's turd. What do you reckon?"

Gareth turned to me, and I could see a smile tugging at the corner of his mouth. "You think so?"

"Yeah. I'm not going to eat any."

"Me neither. And do you know what?"

"What?"

"I'm going to the dam tomorrow and catch more than Jack did."

I frowned at him. "Don't you think you should wait for a week or so?"

"Why?"

"Everybody will have eaten fish tonight. They may not want it again so soon."

"Doesn't matter."

"Give the fish time to recover and breed more."

"Nope."

"I bet your Dad won't take you there tomorrow either. He'll reckon you're just jealous."

Gareth shrugged. "I'll get someone else to take me. Mum, maybe."

I ate the fish of course, and it was fantastic. I even saw Gareth take some.

Then there was a surprise. Meg's car drew up to the main house and she walked over to where we were all grouped at the barbecues. She was smiling and looked younger than I'd seen her for a long time. Her face was softer and she looked happy.

I watched as she made her way to Will and take him aside for a talk. I saw him raise his eyebrows in surprise, but she kept talking until he nodded.

Finally, she walked over to an esky that had been used to store the fish. She went to stand on it, and Will hurried over to help her balance. She clapped her hands together. "Silence!" she called. A hush fell over the crowd. Even the children stopped playing. "I have an announcement."

I knew this would be big. I could feel it in the pit of my stomach. I walked over to my mother and looped my arm through hers. She looked at me and smiled. "Hello Honey-bee," she whispered.

Meg continued. "I have some wonderful news to share with you all. A few weeks ago something extraordinary happened. There was a knock on my door and when I answered, I found William there. The time-traveller has returned."

THEN THERE WERE THREE

Meg's extraordinary announcement caused a chorus of voices to be raised in exclamation. She held a finger to her lips until the noise lessened and then continued. "No more questions now. What I will tell you is that William is an old man in precarious health. He cannot eat our food and I have been trying to adapt what nutrition we have available to his needs. Once this is done successfully, and he feels stronger, I will bring him here to meet you all." She paused and looked around the crowd. "For the time being, I will take his four oldest grandchildren to meet him tonight."

I searched the crowd for Gareth and saw him standing close to Will. His face was lit in excitement. Gone were the dark thoughts caused by Jack's fishing heroics. Everybody had forgotten about that anyway. Now he was going to meet the time traveller.

He didn't turn to look at me, but quickly made his way to the vehicle where Will had begun helping Meg into her seat. Jack, Isabella, and Evie were already clambering in. As the vehicle drove away, all the energy seemed to leave the community. Groups broke away, chatting excitedly among themselves about what this all meant.

I noticed Ruth and Leena standing to one side, looking lost. Although their children were to meet William, the two mothers had been left out. Ruth was holding the hands of her two younger twins. One had its head resting on Ruth's swollen belly where more new life was forming. Sighing, Ruth turned and moved towards her cabin.

My special place in the forest had lost its appeal since being discovered by Gareth. I hadn't found anywhere else, so had adopted the habit of staying on the verandah of the cabin where I rested my notebook on my knee as I scribbled my stories.

On the morning following Meg's announcement, before the settlement began stirring, I closed my eyes in an attempt to take me back into the world I had been writing about. This was a more serious story, one in which a teenage girl was confused about becoming an adult. I began writing and the words flowed quickly. That's when I realised that Gareth was walking towards me with a smile on his face. He looked as though he was in a high state of excitement.

"Hey! Do you wanna hear about my grandfather?"

"Sure. Come and sit down." I patted the bench next to me.

Gareth began talking before his bottom even hit the seat. "He's so cool. Knows all sorts of stuff. So do the others."

"Others?"

"Whoops!" Gareth giggled. "I'm not meant to tell anyone yet. I reckon I can tell you, though."

"Tell me…?"

"There are two more of them."

"Of what?"

"Time travellers." I gasped which made Gareth grin. He was clearly enjoying my reaction.

"Who are they?"

"A guy called Martin. He's old, like William. He had trouble being transported through time. Burns and stuff. Meg and William are worried about him."

"So he's worse than William?"

"Yeah. They think it's because William had some new organs transplanted into him after the last transfer. He was weaker than Martin before they came back here, but did better in the end."

"Gosh. It sounds like time travel is dangerous."

"It is. William was telling us all about it. He said you're

not meant to do it too often. He and Martin shouldn't do it ever again."

"So they can't go back to their own time?"

"They can't anyway. They need a device to trigger the return. Usually it is sent separately within a few hours of transportation. It didn't happen this time, probably because what they were doing was illegal and they were about to get arrested."

I whistled. "Okay, so who is the third guy?"

"Here's where it gets interesting. It's not a guy. It's a girl—or woman I should say—called Grace."

"Really? Wow."

"Yeah, she's some sort of soldier, or something. Very official looking."

"What does she look like? How old is she?"

"She'd be, um, dunno. Twenty-five? She looks a bit like you."

"I can't wait to meet her."

"Well, that's the thing, you see. Martin and Grace don't want to come and live here with the rest of us. They're worried that they'll do things to change the future."

"How?"

"The story goes that when William got Meg pregnant, it changed everything in the future, in their time. Messed it up. They're trying to be careful about anything they do."

"Is that really a thing—that something happens here and the future changes?"

"Yeah, so they reckon. Anyway, Martin and Grace are angry at William because he's already done something…"

I shuffled in my seat in excitement. "What?"

"He fixed India. Cured her. She won't die when she's meant to. Meg made him do it and he didn't check with Martin and Grace first."

"So, how come William is allowed to move here to live with us?"

"Because of Dad and we grandkids—having family here. He's desperate to stay. He promises not to meddle anymore."

"I bet Meg could make him do stuff again. She always gets her way."

Gareth laughed. "Yeah, that's for sure. He also plans to help Will with his projects."

My heart began to beat faster. If Will was to be working with William, then I would as well. How great would that be?

Gareth looked over his shoulder. "I've gotta get back. Mum and Ruth kicked up a fuss last night, so they're going to meet William this morning, and they're taking the younger kids. I'm going too. I want to make something to give to my grandfather."

"Great idea." A thought occurred to me. "You're not going to Lake Baroon, then?"

Gareth looked confused for a moment. Clearly he had forgotten about his vow to catch more fish than Jack. "Oh, fishing? Nah. Too much else to do." He stood and stretched. "I'll see if I can get you in to meet William, hey?" He reached out and touched my hair. "You'd like that, wouldn't you?"

Of course I would, but I wasn't about to let him manipulate me. "Oh, thanks but that's okay. I'm sure I'll get to see him soon."

Gareth pulled his hand away and his face lost its happy glow. "Okay then. See ya later."

I opened my notebook, but couldn't concentrate on my story. Just thinking about the woman time traveller called Grace had taken all thoughts away from what I'd been working on. I thought about what she would be like in looks and personality. A soldier? She would be strong and brave. Time traveller? She would like adventure. How did she come to be in Maleny in 2049? Was there a purpose to her visit?

Fired by imagination, my pen began moving across the page quickly. I began writing the outline of a story about Grace, a fanciful, overblown, action-packed drama which also included a romance. I'd nearly finished drafting this outline, when Ruby, my little sister, poked her head out the door. "Melli! Mum says to come in and help."

I sighed and snapped the notebook closed, my head still full of ideas. The funny thing is that, as unbelievable and exaggerated as this story was, it didn't come even close to the true history of the remarkable woman called Grace.

RUNNING

My father had an important position in the community. He was the manager of the satellite settlement near Nambour, which was referred to as 'The Farm'. This location was used to grow crops—ones that didn't thrive in the unique conditions at Maleny.

This satellite settlement was also responsible for the production of ethanol, vital for fuelling the few remaining internal combustion vehicles, including three tractors, Meg's four-wheel drive, and the people mover which was used for transferring workers to and from The Farm.

The Farm had many buildings: a house, two dormitory-style accommodation units and many sheds for storing machinery and produce. One of the reasons for its selection was that it already had these suitable buildings, as well as the fact it had excellent soil and a good-sized dam.

The older kids from the community, once they had turned thirteen, went to work on The Farm from time to time, along with other, older workers. Most enjoyed the experience and couldn't wait for their next chance to work and stay there. My father allowed the workers some freedoms not normally seen at Maleny, like staying up late and doing some silly things. He thought it was good for them to make mistakes and learn from them, away from the claustrophobic world at Maleny. At the main settlement there was always a parent, or someone else's parent, watching over everything you did.

Gareth had turned thirteen a few months before me and was waiting impatiently for his turn to go and work on The Farm. I wasn't sure that my father was pleased at the prospect. When I raised the subject with him—at Gareth's request—Dad's mouth formed a thin line. "We've never had one of Will's kids there. I don't know how they'll go. There are four of them that have just turned thirteen, so I guess I'll find out." He stopped for a moment and considered the question. "I'm not sure I'll start with Gareth, though. It might be Jack, or one of the girls first."

I decided that telling Gareth this would cause my friend some heartache, so I stayed silent. It didn't take him long to ask me again, though.

"Hey. Now you're thirteen, you'll be able to go to The

Farm, too. We should go at the same time."

"I don't know that my father would agree to that. If you really want to go quickly, perhaps don't mention that idea."

We were due for a rotation of farm workers on the Monday following the announcement about William. What usually happened was that Dad left half the workers at The Farm, and they were watched over by his second-in-charge. The other half were returned to Maleny. Dad would spend two days with us, while selecting the next group. On the Wednesday he would take those workers with him for a month. The workers that were left behind on that occasion would be rotated in two weeks. That meant that we only saw our father for four days out of each month. It never seemed enough.

Zac and I were the oldest in the family, so it was the first time that our father had to consider taking any of his own children to work at Nambour. I was certain that he and my mother would have discussed it at great length, just as I was sure that Zac would get to go before I did.

I didn't see Dad arrive, but heard a stir just before lunch and guessed that he had driven up. I went to the window of Will's workshop in time to see the five teenagers tumble out of the battered people mover. They began unloading produce from the back. Dad was already jogging across the clearing in the direction of our cabin. He always went to see Mum before anything else.

Will came up behind me. "Go and say hi to your Dad. I

won't be starting the next project for a little while. You need lunch anyway."

I flashed him a grateful smile and hung up my lab coat. As I crossed the clearing, I smiled at all the returning farm workers and asked if they'd had a good time away. One of my cousins nodded but said he was starving. He hoped there was some food ready for them.

Dad was sitting at our table with Mum on his knee. He was massaging Mum's swollen belly and talking to her in low tones. As I walked up to them, Mum rested her head on his shoulder.

"Hello there, Melli-Moo. Have you been looking after Mum here?"

"Yeah, but have you heard the news about the time traveller?"

"No. What's happened?"

I gave a quick recap of the events of Saturday night. Dad whistled. "Wow. Things will get a bit interesting around here. I guess I'll miss it all."

"So will the workers who go with you. Maybe they won't be as keen to be selected this time."

Dad's brows raised. "Hmm. You could be right. I'll need to think about that when I make up the new roster."

When Dad left two days later, it was with four older than normal workers and Zac.

I was feeling uncomfortable in my own body. If it wasn't bad enough that I'd sprouted breasts and grown hair in strange places, I had also begun feeling restless, and there was a strange thrumming running right through me which I found unnerving.

This calmed when I'd had lots of activity and then the relief was enormous. I decided to start exercising regularly to see if this helped.

I raided the community clothes store for suitable shoes, socks and clothing. This was disgusting work because the items stored there always seemed to smell bad. The rules stated that all clothing must be freshly washed before being placed in the store, but it seemed that some people cheated. Everything smelled musty, like a teenage boy's bed. There wasn't much in my size, but I rummaged through the piles and took the best of a bad lot.

On the morning following my father's return to Nambour, while the community still slept, I walked to the end of the driveway and considered my options. A left turn would take me along the ridge where there were views of the Glasshouse Mountains, but it would also take me past Meg's house. I was never comfortable with our leader, so my first instinct was to turn right. I began jogging on the spot to keep warm while I tried to make my decision. Maybe, if I went past Meg's house, I'd see one or more of the time travellers. Maybe Meg would find out and get angry with me. I turned right.

The combination of cold air and lack of fitness meant I couldn't run long without finding myself breathless. My chest heaved and I'd have to stop and bend over. I persevered, though, and when I couldn't run, I'd walk fast. I only stayed out for forty-five minutes on my first attempt. The thing was that, by the time I got back to the cabin, I felt great.

By late that afternoon, however, the thrumming was back. I had been sitting in the schoolhouse most of the day and was fidgety. I packed all the books and puzzles into a cupboard and then went to a window. The afternoon was soft and there was a gentle glow rising from the west. I moved quickly to the cabin, changed into my running gear and began making my way past the main community building. As I passed the recreation room, I heard Meg's voice. Her four-wheel drive was parked at the top of the driveway. When I reached the road, I turned left.

I noticed an improvement in my breathing. Maybe it was because of the warmer air. Maybe I'd stretched my lungs in the morning. I felt lighter and happier. This time I was able to run a lot further before stopping to catch my breath.

I had never been inside Meg's house, but knew where it was. Everyone did. It sat high on a hill with the best views in the world. As I jogged past, I wondered if she still appreciated this sight after living there for so many years.

The house seemed quiet. There was no movement that I could see—no time travellers out enjoying the afternoon air. No shadows behind the windows. Nothing stirred.

Past Meg's house the dirt road deteriorated. There had been no reason for the community to keep this section in good repair because it was never used. I cursed as my ankle turned on a pothole and I stopped to assess the damage. It hurt. I sat on the side of the road and rotated the joint. The discomfort eased, so I rose stiffly and began walking again.

I heard somebody approaching before I saw them. There was the sound of running feet thumping on the dirt road ahead of me. As I rounded the corner I saw a sight that stopped me in my tracks. It was a woman running, fast. She had a bandaged eye. The most surprising thing was, however, that she looked just like me.

"Hello," she said, slowing until she was running on the spot. "Who are you?" She gave a half smile.

"Melisandre, from the community. I was exercising."

"Good, but I shouldn't be talking to you. I should go." She didn't move on, though. She stopped moving and looked at me. "You look familiar."

"I think we look alike."

"Yes. I think I looked a lot like you when I was a young teen. How old are you?"

"Just turned thirteen."

"Do you run much?" I noticed the woman's strange speech patterns. The words came out flat, but at high speed.

"I only just started today. It's a bit hard."

"An interesting co-incidence—I began running at about your age. It helped me in all sorts of ways."

I noticed a few details about this woman. Her body was firm and seemingly without fat. I could see every muscle clearly defined in her arms and legs. Her hair was the same colour as mine. It was also long and tied back into a ponytail. Her good eye was the same colour brown as my eyes and was also the same shape.

"What's wrong with your eye? Is it okay?"

"Unknown. It was an unusual injury from time transportation. I don't like looking at it. In a few more days I'll remove the bandages and let William have a look."

"Nasty."

The woman shrugged as if her eye injury were of no consequence. She looked up and down the road. "You didn't seem too surprised to see me. I thought my presence was a secret."

"Gareth knew."

"He told you?"

"Well…yes. He considers me a special friend. He knew I wouldn't tell anybody else."

"So, you haven't told anyone?"

"No, of course not."

"Good girl. I shouldn't be talking to you, though." She looked up the road again. Then seemed to make a decision. She lowered herself until she was sitting on the grass that bordered the road, and leaned against a tree. "Tell me about your friend, Gareth."

"Um…well…we're almost the same age. You've seen him. He has those lovely eyes. Those kids of Will's, they're not always friendly with the rest of us."

"The rest of you?"

"Yeah, well, they're smarter and better looking. They hang out together."

"But not Gareth?"

"No. He's a bit different. I don't think the others like him much. I think he's a bit lonely."

"So he became your friend." She frowned. "Is it a serious friendship? You're at an age…"

I felt the heat rise in my face. The speed of her speech made her questions feel like an interrogation. I sat down next to her. "Gareth has asked to be my boyfriend."

"How do you feel about that?"

"Um, I don't know." I squirmed. "Not ready."

The woman patted my leg. "Good girl. There's no rush, is there?"

"No. My mum says to take my time, make sure I'm okay with it."

"Smart. Listen to her. I'm not sure about Gareth. I've met him twice now. There's something about him…."

"I know what you mean."

"How would you describe it, the thing about him?"

"Um. It's hard to say. It seems like he puts on a front. Tries to prove something. But it comes from insecurity, I think."

"Maybe."

"What do I call you?"

"Grace is my common name. You say your name is

Melisandre? Nice."

"Thank you. It means honey-bee."

The sun was sliding behind a hill. I felt the cool air run its fingers down my warm skin. I shivered. Grace pulled herself to her feet and held out her hand to help me up. She smiled. "I'm not meant to talk to you, but I run morning and night. We might accidentally bump into each other again. I couldn't ignore you, could I?"

I laughed. "No. But I'll keep it a secret."

"Great. It's nice to talk to someone young. The others— William, Meg and Martin—are ancient. And Martin can't talk much."

"Why not?"

"He's too sick. We're afraid we might lose him." Grace shook her legs. "I'd better keep moving. I'll go first…" She stopped and frowned. "You might be able to tell me something."

"Sure. What?"

"Gareth—a fishing trip to Lake Baroon—sometime around now."

"He was going last Sunday, but then there was all the excitement about William coming back…"

Grace dropped her head and kicked at the road. "He didn't go?"

"No. He went to see William with his mother and Ruth."

"That's two things now…"

"Sorry? What two things?"

Grace shook her head. "Just one piece of advice before I go—"

"Yeah?"

"Gareth. Trust your instincts about him. There are things I know…" Grace turned and began running, waving as she went.

Gareth sidled up to me and spoke out of the corner of this mouth. "Martin didn't make it."

"He's dead?"

"Yeah. They tried everything. William is really upset. Like really bad."

I had wondered why I hadn't seen Grace on my runs in the two days since I'd first met her. Now I knew. Everything would have been turned upside down at Meg's house.

"That's so sad."

"It changes things."

"Like what?"

"The plan was for Martin and Grace to live apart from the community—find a way to be self-sufficient. We kids, the oldest four of William's grandkids, were going to help them. Now that can't happen."

"It would be awful to live alone under those circumstances."

"Yeah. Grace is still insisting that it's too dangerous for her to live among us, though. She says they've already made too much of an impact."

"I wonder what that means?"

"India, for one."

I thought about Grace's comment when she heard that Gareth didn't go fishing. Somehow this was significant. "I hope she comes and lives with us, anyway. It would be cool."

"Yeah. I find that eye thing creepy, though."

I was about to comment on that, about how William might be able to help repair the damage to her eye, but realised that would alert Gareth to the fact I'd met Grace. I just nodded. "Maybe it will get better."

"Maybe. Hey, I haven't seen you much lately. Do ya wanna hang out? We could slip away later today for a while."

I turned and looked at Gareth's eager face and noticed a sense of over-excitement, the same as I saw that morning in the forest. The way he looked at me made the hairs on the back of my neck stand up. I remembered Grace's words and placed trust in my instincts.

"Can't do. Mum and Dad have said I'm not allowed to be alone with any boys."

"But I'm not just any boy. I'm your friend." He looked disappointed. "C'mon. It'll be okay. We'll just hang out."

"Well…"

"Nobody needs to know. Nothing bad will happen." He flashed his charismatic smile then—the one that he knew could tip the balance in his favour. "Trust me."

That was the thing, you see. Our friendship had changed. I didn't trust him, and Grace knew something she wasn't telling me.

"No. Mum and Dad would freak out if they knew. If you want to hang out, it needs to be here."

Gareth's smile vanished and he turned away. For a second I saw how flushed his face had become. It was dark with anger. He didn't like being refused.

I guessed I was losing my special, sparkly-eyed friend.

THE STRANGER

"Tell me about living here, in this limited world of yours."
Grace was looking at me quizzically. This wasn't small talk, it
was genuine interest and need to know.

"It's okay, I guess. Well it's all we've got."

"And I suppose you don't know what to miss, because
you weren't alive before the pandemic."

I nodded. "True, but we see books and things. We know
what life was like before."

"Well, what's the worst part of living now?"

"Seeing the same people day after day. That's why the
whole settlement is in a state of excitement about seeing
William, because to most people, he is a *new face!*"

Grace smiled. "They'll certainly welcome me then."

"You're coming to live with us!"

"Yes, there isn't really any other option."

I wriggled on the bench. "That will be so cool."

"Will you help me?"

"How?"

Grace was silent for a moment. We were sitting in a park that had been overtaken by sub-tropical vegetation. It had taken us a few minutes to clear the benches so we could sit and talk in comfort.

"Just be there for me. It will take some adjustment." She looked at me. "Just be my friend."

I wondered about this. Grace seemed so self-possessed and capable. I thought she would be able to handle herself in any situation. Why did she need me? In any case, I was happy with her request. I liked Grace and she was really interesting.

"Sure. I'll be there for you."

I asked her about life in the future. She quickly told me about the normal things: housing, food, transportation and entertainment. When I said it sounded wonderful, she shook her head. "It wasn't, you know. It was a bad world, run by a bad man."

"Who was that?"

"The Emperor. He was cruel and greedy. His sanity was in doubt."

"Wow. Did he do anything bad to you?"

"Me personally? Yes. Terrible things to my family. I will

tell you about them another day." I saw her sadness and decided to change the subject.

"How many children do you have? Lots by now, I guess?"

Grace smiled. "No. It's not like here. I don't have any yet."

"Really? I can't imagine that. I thought you'd have six or more by now."

"No, and at this rate I may not have any at all."

"Did you have a boyfriend?"

"Yes, but that's another sad story. The man I love, Caelius, he…well he may not still be alive. There were things happening just as I left." I saw her good eye moisten. "There was someone else I was seeing as well—Caelius knew about this. I was seeing him to get information because he was close to the Emperor. He wanted to marry me."

"What was his name?"

"Valerius."

"Were you going to? Marry him, I mean?"

Grace's good eye had a faraway look. "He cared for me in his strange way, but I didn't love him."

"Would you go back to your own time, if you could?"

"Not until I fix things here first."

"How do you mean?"

Grace shook her head and straightened her spine. "Sorry. Talking about the past made me talk nonsense. I don't believe it is an option for me to return to that time, but if I could—I just don't know. I left there at a time when some terrible things were happening to the people I loved. I didn't mean to come here—I was trying to save William and got caught up in it."

"Gosh!"

Grace smiled and changed the subject. "What's the one thing you would have liked to do in the time before the pandemic?"

"That's easy. Fly in a plane! Imagine what that must be like!"

"Yes, it is special. We might be able to build something, you know. A small, light aircraft."

"You're kidding me."

"No. It's not hard. William would be able to advise us."

I shook my head in wonder. "How good would that be?"

"The other thing…I've noticed your shoes. They're no good for running. You'll do damage to yourself."

I looked at Grace's shoes. "Where did yours come from?"

"Meg took us to a place, a warehouse. There was sporting equipment and other things. The hardest part was finding running shoes that hadn't perished with time. I grabbed a few pairs. What size shoe are you?"

"Eight and a half."

"Great. That's the same as me. When I come over to the settlement, I'll bring you a pair."

"When are you coming?"

"William and I will move over there quite soon. He's eating okay now and I think Meg wants her house back to herself."

I laughed in delight. "Everyone will be so excited!"

The schoolhouse was crowded and felt airless. I stretched my arms above my head and looked over to see what Heather was doing. She was talking to Will's daughters, and showing them something on a chart. The girls looked bored. I checked the clock. Still an hour until we broke for afternoon tea. Time was moving slowly.

I noticed little Toby yawning, so thought it a good idea to give him a task.

"I think we need more air in here. Toby, would you help me by opening the two windows by the door?"

Toby shot out of his seat and ran towards the front of the room. A few minutes later, I found him at my elbow, tugging on my overalls.

"Melli. Melli."

I ignored him for a moment while answering Kate's question. Then I turned and said, "What is it, Toby?"

His eyes were huge. "A man, dressed funny."

"Where?"

"Coming up the driveway."

I moved the boy to one side and walked to the door. Male voices, loud ones, were echoing across the settlement. One belonged to my grandfather, Luke, but I didn't know the other. From behind the door, where I couldn't be seen by the men, I lowered myself to my knees and inched forward until I could see through the lower half of the window.

The stranger wore a uniform I had never seen before. It

was made from a dark cloth that looked heavy. The shirt was a crisp white. He wore knee-length boots. A pert hat, which seemed to defy gravity, sat on one side of his head.

Compared to Luke, who worked mostly outdoors and was still muscular despite his advancing years, the stranger appeared pale and slight. From what I could see of his hair, under the hat, he was prematurely grey.

Their words were indistinct until Luke raised his voice with a tone of frustration. "I told you, there is nobody of that name here."

The stranger straightened his shoulders. "And I'm telling you she wouldn't be anywhere else."

"Well, I haven't seen her."

"What about an old man called William?" The words came quickly, in a flat tone.

Luke raised his hands in exasperation. "Look, you really have to speak to Meg, our leader. I'll send someone to get her."

"She doesn't live here?"

"No, but she's not far away." Luke looked around the crowd that had gathered, trying to find someone suitable to send for Meg. He shook his head. "There's nobody here right now—"

I chewed my lip. Who was this man? His speech patterns were similar to Grace's, and it seemed like he might be looking for her. I remembered what Grace told me about having to leave her time quickly to save William. Did the appearance of this man mean she was now in danger?

I stepped out of the schoolroom and made my way to the two men. "Hey Grandad. I can run to Meg's. It won't take long."

Luke gave me a smile of relief. "Thanks, Melli."

I turned to the stranger and saw his eyes for the first time. They were like Will and Gareth's. "Who can I say wants to see her?"

The man looked puzzled for a moment. "Oh, I see. I am Valerius."

Valerius. I'd heard that name before, from Grace. Was he the love of her life, or the other who wanted to marry her? I tried to remember exactly what she had said.

"And what can I say you wish to discuss with her?"

The man puffed his chest out. "Just get her, will you? I am here on official business."

I didn't like the way he issued orders to me. Who did he think he was? This couldn't be the man Grace loved.

My overalls were horrid to run in, as were the shoes I was wearing, but I knew this was an emergency. I had to warn Grace. Each footfall of that run up to Meg's house chafed my thighs and made the straps of the overalls rub over my shoulders in an unpleasant way. I kept sliding out of the shoes.

At last Meg's house came within sight and I had my first moments of panic. What would I say to Meg? I should have thought it through.

I knocked on the timber door and tried to look through the frosted glass of the side panels. Finally, I could see a shadow approaching. I prayed it would be my new friend.

Meg's face appeared. When she saw me, she frowned. "Yes?"

"Luke sent me. It's urgent."

"What is?"

"A man has arrived. A stranger. He is asking about William, and also a woman." I raised my voice slightly. "He said his name was Valerius."

I heard an object being dropped in another room of the house. Clearly my message had been received.

"I see. Yes, I will come immediately. Wait for me in my car."

I walked slowly to the white four-wheel-drive, my ears cocked in case I could hear Meg talking to anybody. She appeared after a few minutes and climbed into the driver's seat.

"Tell me what this man is like."

"He's wearing a full uniform of some sort. He talks with a strange speech pattern…" I nearly said, 'like Grace's', but caught myself in time. "He talks quickly and the words are flat. He is pale and not well-built. He seems important."

Meg started the motor and we began moving. "What did Luke tell him?"

"That he didn't know of the woman he was asking about."

"What about William? Did Luke say he knew of him?"

"No, he just said that the man would have to talk to you."

"I wonder…" Meg's voice became distant as she lapsed into deep thought. She remained silent until we arrived at the settlement.

The man called Valerius was inside the original community house, looking through the shelves of CDs and DVDs. Some children had escaped the schoolhouse and were watching him through the glass, giggling from time to time. There were adults, too, peering through the windows. Excitement shimmered in the air.

Meg brushed down her dress, which was faded and worn, before entering the house. I felt awkward, not knowing what I should do. Should I go with her, or back to the schoolhouse? I decided to follow her—she could always tell me to go away.

"You wanted to see me?" Meg's bearing and tone were quite regal.

Valerius turned. His eyes flickered over her clothing. "I've come to make two arrests as well as effect a rescue. I need to find three time travellers. Their names are William, Martin and Aelia.

"I see. What makes you think they are here?"

Valerius' eyes narrowed. "I have conducted years of research on being able to tell if a person is lying. Beware of this."

Meg laughed. "You're threatening me!"

"I am here on official business. I represent the Emperor."

"Listen, sonny. You may or may not be on official business, but let me tell you something. You have no authority here. I am the leader. If you threaten me, you will be dealt with. There is one of you, but a great many of us." She was breathing quickly. "And let me tell you, the men here are in a lot bigger and fitter than you."

Valerius' mouth opened and closed several times. I could see his Adam's apple bobbing up and down. "Look here—"

Meg spoke over him. "So you can ask nicely for my co-operation or you can just go away. It's up to you."

Valerius stared at Meg for a few moments, then dropped his gaze to the floor. "The girl, Aelia. She was transported accidentally. She is a member of the militia. I've come to take her back."

"I'll return to my original question. What makes you think they are here?"

"The time technician was told to send them here. The same man then sent me to the same co-ordinates, as soon as the portal re-opened."

"Portal?"

"Oh, it's complicated. There was a delay."

Meg weighed his words for a moment. "So, this William you're talking about. You're going to arrest him?"

Valerius shrugged. "Yes…no…I'm not sure. That's not important. I just want to return with Aelia, to our own time." His voice lowered, slowed down. "Is she here?"

"No, she's not here, but I know where she is. We thought it too dangerous to let the time travellers have much to do with this community."

"So, where is she?"

"I'll let you know in due course." Meg turned and seemed surprised to see me standing there. "This girl will take you to one of the sheds that has a bathroom and a bed. She will arrange food. I'll go and talk to Aelia. I'll come back tonight. After dark."

Meg nodded at me and walked out the sliding doors which led to the verandah and beyond to the car park. I looked at the stranger and he stared back expectantly. It was then I realised I'd just been made responsible for him. "Follow me," I said without enthusiasm.

The day Valerius arrived wasn't a Sunday, so there was no formal dinner. Children were fed early, an hour before the adults. When it came time for the second sitting, members of the community wandered through the common room, casually, helping themselves to whatever food was laid out on the tables which hugged the western wall. Restraint was always shown at these times, and we had been taught from a young age to only take what we could eat. There was to be no waste.

One table was always reserved for the elders who were Luke, Connie, George, Heather, India and Meg. Sometimes

Will sat at this table if there were discussions that required his attention. Connie rarely attended.

By the time dinner was served on this night, Meg still had not returned to talk to the stranger. I stood, looking around the tables, and realised I had no idea what I was meant to do with Valerius. Should I bring him for a meal? I was only thirteen years old—what did I know of these things? I noticed that a lot of people were watching me and murmuring among themselves. It made me feel nervous. I walked out.

Will would know what to do. I ran from building to building looking for him. Ruth said he had gone out earlier and not returned. I found Grandfather Luke who shrugged and said I should do what I felt was best. Gareth came up to me puffing and with a red face—he had been away with Jack sending up weather balloons for his father—and wanted to know all about the newcomer. I said I couldn't stop to talk because Meg had given me urgent instructions.

I thought hard. Valerius was from the future. Grace believed that time travellers could cause harm. The best scenario, therefore, was one where the stranger was kept from the general population. Once I decided this, I was happier.

I returned to the shed where Valerius was sitting on the bed, staring at a strange device. He would shake it and slap it with the palm of his hand. Then he would stare at it again and the process would start all over again.

"Are you hungry? I'll get you some dinner."

Valerius simply grunted and kept staring at the device.

"What do you want? I think they have meat tonight. Salad? Vegetables?"

The man looked at me with irritation. I stared back at him, annoyed. Didn't he know I was trying to help him?

"Just get me food—I don't care what—and lower your eyes when you talk to me. Understand?"

I felt a flash of anger. "What? Why?"

"Why what?"

"Why do I have to lower my eyes?"

"It looks like I'll have to teach you people a thing or two." He slapped the device in his hands. "Just get me some food. Now!"

Anger made me misbehave.

Our community was run on the principle that there was no excuse for outright rudeness. Valerius' attitude, therefore, made it feel like a bucket of cold water had been poured over me, such was the shock of being spoken to like that. Lower my eyes? What was that about?

I didn't take food to Valerius quickly. I went to the common room and filled my own plate, taking time with choices. I fielded questions about the stranger. I ate slowly, chewing every mouthful until it was liquid in my mouth.

Only then did I find a tray and return to the food tables.

The selection for Valerius was nothing like my own. I half-filled the plate with broccoli, a vegetable I couldn't even stand the smell of. I added celery, radishes and Brussels sprouts. I bypassed bread and eggs, chicken and sweetcorn. I noticed George's favourite extra strong mustard and drizzled some over the whole plate. Satisfied, I returned to the shed, and passed the tray to the stranger. He looked at the food and then at me. I stared back into his eyes, crossed my arms and made my lips thin. Valerius sighed and picked up the fork. Soon he was chewing the food with distaste.

I took a chair outside and sat near the entrance to the shed. There was enough light to write by, so I began the last chapter of my book—the one about the Boo-gang. I planned to finish it before bedtime, so I could test the first couple of chapters on my siblings that night.

I only got to write a few sentences before I noticed a strange sight. Walking toward the shed, being supported by Meg, was Grace. The reason she needed support was that both her eyes were bandaged. I wanted to leap to my feet and run to her—ask what was wrong—but realised that would be a mistake. I sat silently and watched their approach.

I think Meg would have walked straight past me, but Grace sensed my presence. "Who is there?" she asked.

"Melisandre. Meg asked me to sort things for the stranger."

"So, you are the girl who ran to Meg's this afternoon to let us know of Valerius' arrival?"

I smiled to myself. "Yes, that was me."

"Thank you for that. My name is Aelia. I'd like to talk to you later, if that's alright?"

"Yes, of course."

The two women made their way into the shed. I stayed outside but could hear every word.

"Aelia? Aelia—oh, what's happened? What's wrong with your eyes?"

"Valerius, is that you? Oh, it's so good to have you here. Have you come to take me home?"

"Yes, of course. I couldn't just let you be stranded here. I've missed you."

"Oh, and I've missed you. I've been so miserable."

I frowned. These words sounded false to me. Even Grace's tone of voice was different—higher and sort of breathless.

"I'll take you back as soon as we can be transported. But tell me, what happened to your eyes?"

"They were damaged during transportation."

"I've never heard of that happening."

"Martin, poor old Martin, thought it might be because I'm a woman. There has never been a female time traveller. Difference in physiological make up and all that…"

"Yes, I see. But it seems strange. I had absolutely no effect from transportation. I didn't like it, but I just felt a bit hot."

"You're lucky. Poor Martin had travelled too many times and didn't make it."

Listening to these two talk made my head spin. Both of them spoke so quickly that it was hard to follow the words.

There was almost no expression used, no variation in tone. I snuck a look around the edge of the door frame. Meg was watching Valerius and Grace and frowning.

Valerius continued his questioning. "What about William. How is he?"

"Not good. He may not survive. We'll know more in the next few days."

This was news to me. I thought he was doing well. What a fascinating conversation this was turning out to be.

"Will your eyes recover?"

"Unknown. The damage is severe. My right eye, the best of the two has turned brown—"

"What? You're not serious?"

"Would I joke about something like that? The left eye is still the normal colour, but severely damaged. I think I've completely lost my sight."

"Poor darling. But the brown-eye—that's awful. We'll have to get that fixed somehow when we get back home."

"Yes, of course."

"Can you see anything at all?"

"Only shadows from the right eye. That's why it's bandaged. I'm trying to give it every chance to recover."

"Are you alright, otherwise?"

"Just very weak. I can't stand for long, my legs give out. I can only stay for a few minutes. I don't want to jeopardise my recovery by getting too tired."

"Sit here, on the bed. That way you'll be able to stay a

bit longer. I'll just move the Pigeon device. I tried to send a report to the Commander, but the device isn't working."

"I don't think it will while you're here. Yes, I will sit, thank you. Tell me what happened after I was transported. What did the Emperor say?"

"He threw a fit. A real fit. One of his tantrums."

Grace was silent for a moment. Her next words were said quietly and with hesitation. "And what about your brother—his fight to the death with that Insurgent—"

Valerius coughed. "I didn't see the fight myself, but it has gone down as the toughest in history."

"What happened?" Grace sounded like she was talking from a great distance.

"Both dead."

"Oh…oh no. How?"

"Apparently they both fought and fought for way longer than their bodies could possibly be expected to survive. My brother had the greater skill, but Caelius had what they're calling an 'indomitable will". He just wouldn't die."

"So, how did it end?"

"They both struck death blows at the same time. Both died instantly."

"What a waste. A terrible waste."

"Yes, my brother will be missed. No sad loss of the brown-eye, though."

Grace was silent. I heard Valerius move. "Poor darling. You look shattered. I've kept you here too long. Let Meg take you back to where you're staying. Where is that, by the way?"

Grace didn't respond. Meg ended the silence. "Just up the road a way. I'll bring Aelia back when she's feeling better. It may be a couple of days."

"That long? How disappointing. I could come and help look after her."

"That's not necessary. We've got that covered."

I heard some shuffling as the two women made their way to the door. As she reached me, Grace put her spare arm around my shoulders so that she could lean on me as we made their way back to the vehicle. I opened the door for her. She whispered, "Come and see me tomorrow. I'll make sure it's alright with Meg. Around ten o'clock, okay?"

I nodded. I couldn't wait.

As I watched Meg drive away, I realised she hadn't issued me with any instructions about Valerius. Was I meant to watch him? Keep him away from the rest of the community? Clearly the man didn't like me and the feeling was mutual. I wanted to be as far away from him as I could.

A shadow approached silently and I could make out the shape of Gareth. Unlike his siblings who were slightly-built, he carried weight around his stomach and backside, making his silhouette resemble a pear with legs.

"Hey. What's happening?"

I put my finger to my lips and led him away from the

shed. "This guy came looking for the time travellers. His name is Valerius."

"So, what has that got to do with you?"

"Meg put me in charge of him."

"Why?"

"Just because I was standing there, I think."

"What do you have to do?"

"Meg didn't really say. I'm just keeping an eye on him."

"What's he like?"

"Different. He thinks Grace's name is Aelia, by the way. You should know that in case he talks to you."

"Ah, okay."

"Oh, and we have to say that William is really sick. And both of Grace's eyes were damaged."

"Sounds complicated. Do you have to stay here all night?"

"I don't know. Meg told me to look after him, but I don't know what to do now. I think he needs to be kept separate from the rest of the community."

"Yeah, I reckon that would be right. Why didn't Meg take him with her?"

"That's a big question. I get the feeling that he is a threat—an enemy."

"Oh."

Valerius' figure loomed in the doorway of the shed. "Who's there?" I heard Gareth swallow.

"Gareth. Meg's grandson."

"Come here for a moment."

Gareth gave me a startled look before moving to the light of the shed. I heard Valerius grunt. "That's better. I'd like you to look after me instead of this brown-eye."

"What?"

"You're Elite. I don't want that girl anywhere near me."

"Elite?"

Valerius sighed. "Are you all stupid? Listen, get me some decent food, would you? And I need you to show me how the waste disposal works."

"The what?"

"In the back there."

"The toilet?"

"Whatever. But food first. I'm very hungry."

Gareth stood still for a moment as if wondering how to answer this rude man. He finally turned and began walking toward the kitchens. I followed.

"Nasty piece of work, isn't he?" I said.

"Hmm. And what's that thing about the eyes?"

"It's come up a few times now. I'm not sure. He certainly seems to prefer you to me. Do you mind looking after him?"

"Nah, it's sort of cool. Even if he is rude. I reckon I could find out some interesting stuff."

"I don't think you're meant to have much to do with him. Be careful what you tell him—it looks as though saying the wrong thing might put William and Grace in danger."

"Sure. You'd better go and let your Mum know where you are. She'll be needing your help."

I smiled. It was nice when Gareth was thoughtful. I touched him on the arm. "Thanks. See you later, alligator."

He flashed me a smile. "In a while, crocodile."

THE WORLD GRACE LEFT

"I'm so glad to see you. Come over here." Grace took me by the arm and led me to the pier that jutted out onto the dam next to Meg's house.

She had obviously been watching for me, because I'd only just entered the driveway from the road when I saw her walk out the front door. Only one eye was bandaged and the other, brown one, looked normal.

There were two chairs on the pier, and Grace waved me into one of them.

I sat and looked over the water. It was a pretty dam, with green grass running down to the edge on all sides. The birds seemed to delight in it, skimming the surface time and time again. The whole scene made me feel peaceful.

Grace wasn't at peace. She began pacing, talking rapidly.

"I need your help, Melisandre. An ally. You're the only person I feel I can trust here."

"Of course you can trust me. What about Meg?"

"No. Ultimately she and I will oppose each other. I will have to do something—probably a number of things—that she won't like. She'll fight me if she has the chance."

"Gosh. What sort of things?"

"I'll tell you later. For now, I've asked Meg if you could be my companion—visit me from time to time."

"What did she say?"

"She said, 'What does everybody see in that girl?'"

I laughed. "Yes, that about sums it up."

"Anyway, she's sort of agreed for the time being. Listen, I feel a bond with you. A strange bond. We look alike and there are other things. We have the same shoe size. You remind me of myself when I was younger. I wonder if you are an ancestor of mine, or something?"

"Wow. That would be cool."

Grace smiled. "Indeed. There is so much to tell you, I don't know where to begin. What you have to understand, though, is that nobody in this time knows all of this. William knows some of it and I've sworn him to secrecy."

"Oh, okay."

Grace sat down then, and took my hands in hers. "You know my eyes are naturally brown, don't you? Like yours?"

"Yes."

"Valerius thinks they're like his. I wore special coloured lenses, and one was still in my eye when I was transported, which is what caused the damage. The lens fused onto my eye from the heat."

"Oh, gosh."

"I have to pretend that my eyes are Elite eyes. Colourful like his. Get it?"

"Yes, but why?"

Grace spent the next hour talking rapidly, telling me about the terrible world she'd escaped from and her reasons for it. She told me about the mad Emperor who made the lives of the subclass, the brown-eyes, miserable.

I nodded. "Valerius told me I couldn't look at him."

"Yes, that's what it's like. We're not much better than animals to him."

I felt anger and resentment welling again. "He's so rude!"

"Yes. I know. Anyway, there are things I can do back in this time to make sure this never happens in my time—that it never did."

"Really?"

"See, it should never have happened in the first place. William caused it when he got Meg pregnant. It changed everything."

I whistled. Wow. "So how do you fix it?"

Grace looked away. "I'm working on that. I'll let you know."

"So Valerius knows nothing about this?"

"No. We have to keep him in the dark. Make him think that William is near death and that I'm weak and blind. That will give me the chance to work on my own agenda."

"Sure. How do we keep Valerius out of trouble back at the community house?"

"I'll leave that to Meg. She can instruct Will. I don't want you anywhere near Valerius. He'll treat you very badly."

"I'm glad you think that way. He requested that Gareth look after him last night. It was a better arrangement all 'round."

Grace frowned and then smiled. "That's funny. Good. You can go back to the community now—be my eyes and ears there. Come back tomorrow would you? Same time."

"I guess you can't go running anymore, in case Valerius sees you."

"Exactly, and it's killing me."

My head was pounding with all the information Grace had given me. Her world sounded terrible. She was so brave, pretending to be Elite and living in their world of entitlement and luxury, taking Valerius as a lover to get information from him. It made me feel so sad that her real love, Caelius, had been killed by Valerius' brother. Poor Grace.

I decided I would be like her. Brave, a warrior. I would help her in the fight to free her people. I felt strong and powerful. We would do this together, sisters in war.

As I helped in the schoolhouse that afternoon, my mind wouldn't stop asking one question. What could Grace possibly do in this world to save her people in the other one?

THE BET

"Hello Melli-belly!" My father gave me a squeeze. "Gosh, you're growing up. You're looking well, too."

"I'm running a lot."

"Good, good. Ah, it's great to be home. I'll go and say hello to your mother before anything else."

Zac pushed past me, carrying a box of vegetables. He didn't look happy. I ran after him. "Hey, how was The Farm? You're back early."

"Yeah, it's okay. Hard to have Dad watching over me, though."

"I guess that's tough."

"Yeah, the other guys got to muck around a lot, but I

wasn't always included because of who I was. Dad said two weeks was long enough for my first time."

I felt sorry for him. That must have been rough. I decided to cheer him up. "At least you're back now. Stuff has been happening and it's all about to get interesting."

Zac stopped walking and looked at me. "Like what?" I told him an edited version of events. The arrival of Valerius a week ago, and how Gareth was looking after him.

"Wow. So William isn't here?"

"No, Valerius wants to arrest him, so Meg told him that William's really sick. Might die." I didn't mention Grace.

"Where is he now, the stranger?"

"He spends most of his time in the shed. He's interested in our music and movies. Old music. Gareth set up a player for him. He always wears full uniform—insists that Gareth find workers to wash and iron his shirts."

Zac laughed. "What, and they do it?"

"Yeah. I wouldn't."

"What have you found out about him?"

"Nothing."

"Haven't you talked with him?"

"No. He's not the talkative type."

"That's just because you're a girl. He probably thinks you're dumb."

I whacked Zac across the arm. "Don't be rude."

"I bet *I* could find out stuff."

I was just about to tell him that he shouldn't be talking to the stranger, when I looked into his eyes. That gave me an idea. It made me smile.

"Okay, what will you bet?"

"What?"

"What will you bet me that you can find out more from Valerius?"

"Um, dunno."

"How about this—if I win, you take on one of my jobs for a week. Maybe laundry."

"And if I win?"

"I take on one of yours."

Zac smiled broadly "Like collecting the cow and horse shit for fertiliser?"

That made me pause for a moment, but then I smiled. "Yeah. Done."

"Great. I'll go and see him right now. You wait—I'll find out all sorts of stuff."

"Go for it."

Zac handed me the box of vegetables and ran over to the shed. I saw him say something to Gareth, and then move toward the doorway.

Little Amelia ran up to me with her face shining like sunbeams, and asked about my new book. When would it be ready? I crouched down and tidied her hair so it sat back in its ponytail. I answered her question and then couldn't help but give her a tickle under the armpits, just so I could hear her laugh. As I stood, I noticed Zac walking back towards me. His face was dark. He snatched the box back from me and said, "Rude prick."

"Who?"

"That idiot in uniform. What a bastard."

"What did he say?"

"Said I couldn't talk to him. He didn't believe in making conversation with brown-eyes."

I smiled. The fact that Valerius wasn't making friends in our community was a positive. "Laundry it is then. A whole week!"

Zac's face was like a thundercloud. "That's not fair!"

"What isn't? It's a bet, fair and square."

"We didn't shake on it!"

"Too bad. You still accepted the bet."

My twin was clearly unhappy. He turned and strode towards the cabin. Amelia tugged on my sleeve. "Melli. Come to my house. Come and see my new bed!"

"Okay, but I can only stay a few minutes."

Amelia took my hand and dragged me to the cabin where Will, Ruth and their children lived. Somehow Will had arranged for an extension on his cabin, despite the fact that he and Ruth had fewer children than my parents did. There was also a nice area at the back, leading off the kitchen, where the family could eat outside when the weather permitted.

As we entered the cabin through the front door, I could hear voices coming from the back. As Amelia led me to her new bed, I could hear Ruth talking to her mother, India.

"Leena's getting worse. Talks to herself more. It's like she hears voices that nobody else can hear."

"You're not exaggerating are you?"

"No. Absolutely not, Mum. Listen, now that you're well again, now that the cancer is gone, you'll have to start watching her yourself."

"I suppose so."

"It's Bella I worry about most."

"You're not concerned about Gareth?"

"In a different way. He's just like Leena, but Bella isn't. It must be hard for her to live in that cabin."

Amelia was pulling at me. "Look, Melli. Mum made me a new quilt cover. Isn't it pretty?"

"Oh, just beautiful."

I heard India's voice again. "What do you think we should do about Bella?"

"Ask her if she wants to move. She could live with you, maybe."

"Not much fun for a girl her age."

"She could come here, I guess. She is Will's daughter after all."

Amelia opened a wooden chest and began hauling toys out of it. She wanted to show me everything.

Ruth continued. "Maybe we could get her sent to The Farm for a month, then decide what to do after that."

"Good idea. I'll talk to Trent. Maybe he'll take her back with him on Wednesday."

"Where did this come from, Mum? Why are Leena and Gareth like this?"

"I've wondered about that. My auntie, that is my father's sister, suffered from mental illness most of her adult life."

"Really? Do you know what type?"

"No, it wasn't something that was discussed a great deal. I know she was institutionalised—considered a danger to herself and others. Worse than Leena. What we have to take into account, though, is that your sister is still a young woman. We don't know how much worse it will get."

The two women stopped talking. I helped Amelia pack her toys back into the chest with a heavy heart. Poor Leena and Gareth. Is that what Grace knew? Was Gareth more than just a bit weird?

After having dinner with my family, I dropped past the shed to see how things were with Valerius. Gareth was sitting outside the door, in the same chair that I had placed there. He had a large book on his lap and was fully engrossed in it.

"Psst! Hey, Gareth."

"Hey Melli. What are you up to?"

I looked at my friend and wondered exactly what his own family saw about him that caused concern. Yes, he was spoiled and threw tantrums, although I'd never witnessed one. He was restless and had trouble with concentrating for any length of time. Then there were the new vibrations

I was getting from him, aggressive in a physical way that I wasn't comfortable with. That didn't mean he was bonkers. I could see that his mother had problems, could definitely be a suffering a mental illness, but not Gareth.

"Just thought I'd drop by and see how you were going. Do you want me to find someone to relieve you?"

"Nah. I'm happy here. I've got a new book that Meg loaned me from that great set of shelves at her house."

"Have you eaten?"

"Yeah. I got him some too." Gareth tossed his head in the direction of the inside of the shed, from where fast-paced violin music was floating.

"Great."

"Hey, what do you know about ancient Rome?"

"Um. Not much. Julius Caesar and all that. Aqueducts. Coliseums."

"Everybody talks so much about Julius Caesar, but there were lots of cool dude rulers back then."

"Really?"

"Yeah, and they were like, amazing. I wish I lived back then."

"Ha, well…with all this time travel—"

"If only. Wow. Wouldn't that be just awesome. Hey, look at these buildings. I love the Forum."

I looked over Gareth's shoulder. One of the images was a photograph of the ruins, while the other was a drawing of how the building looked in its heyday.

"Impressive."

The music in the shed stopped. I heard movements as Valerius opened a new CD case. Softer music began filtering out. There were more steps before a shadow fell across Gareth and his book.

Valerius' words came in their strange flat manner. "What do you have there, boy?"

"Just a book that Meg loaned me."

"I need books. Can you get me some?"

"Sure. What sort?"

"Something with stories. Interesting ones. Maybe true stories that happened before 2013."

"I'll find something tomorrow."

"What's your book about?"

"Not stories. Just history. Ancient Rome."

Something changed in the air. I felt it, but it was beyond description. Valerius fell silent for ten seconds or so.

"Who did you say you were? Who are your parents?" His words arrived like bullets.

"My father is Will; my mother is Leena." Gareth was squirming in his seat.

"And who are their parents?"

I was still partially hidden from Valerius, enough to give Gareth a kick on his foot.

"Um. India…um…dunno about the rest."

Valerius was gone, back into the shed, but I heard him pacing until I left and went back to my cabin.

Grace's good eye was wide with surprise.

"And Valerius didn't say another word to Gareth?"

"Not before I left, anyway."

"Interesting. I wonder how long it will take him…"

"To do what?"

Grace looked at me levelly. "Work out his lineage."

"Who, Gareth's?"

"Hmm. He might end up doing some of my work for me, if we're lucky."

"And what work—"

"I'm still trying to figure that one out. What else has been happening in the community?"

"Well, not much since I saw you yesterday. Well, I heard a sad conversation."

"About what?"

"Leena and Gareth."

"Tell me."

I recounted the conversation between India and Ruth. Grace listened and weighed every word, sometimes asking for clarification. When I finished she just nodded. "I'm going to tell you something, just because I trust you so much. Okay?"

I wondered what was coming. "Sure."

"Leena should have died by now."

I felt the blood drain from my face. "What do you mean?"

"When Gareth's half-brother, what's his name, Jack?" I nodded. "When Jack caught all those fish, and a big fuss was made…"

"Yeah?"

"Gareth was going fishing the next morning. The Sunday."

"Yes, I remember you asking me about that."

"What should have happened was that nobody would take him to the dam, so he threw a tantrum. His mother agreed to supervise his driving a tractor there. There was an accident, caused by him—he hit the accelerator instead of the brake, then swerved. The tractor tipped into the dam, trapping Leena under a wheel. Gareth watched his mother drown, and it was an awful death."

I listened in horror. "I'm so glad that didn't happen!"

Grace pulled her chair around so she was facing me squarely. "But don't you see, the reason it didn't happen was that we arrived. We've changed things already. I don't know what this will mean back in our time."

"So, it's like you said. This is the second thing. The first was saving India's life."

"That's right"

"But there's still something you're not telling me, isn't there?"

"Yes."

"What is it?"

"As soon as I work it out, I'll tell you in detail, I promise. I'm just not sure yet."

"But I can tell, the focus is on Gareth. He has something to do with what was going on in your time. He is in this world because William got Meg pregnant. Everyone is talking about his sanity…"

"Yes, but we don't know what it all means yet."

I knew she did, but didn't want to tell me just now. She needed me to be her eyes and ears so she could work out a plan. It had to do with Gareth. She knew Gareth was a friend of mine. I could tell she thought I wasn't ready—not emotionally mature enough—for the truth. I decided that was okay. I'd have to prove myself so we could be sisters in the fight for her cause. Warrior sisters.

That's what I would do. I would go back to the community and, not only find out what Grace needed to know, but I would also discover what the mystery was. What significance was Gareth to the future world? How could a slightly mixed-up thirteen-year-old boy cause such misery in hundreds of years' time?

This is what I would find out, and in the process, I would prove myself to Grace.

TITUS OF ANCIENT ROME

It became my habit to listen to every conversation I could hear in the community so that I could pass the information on to Grace. Nothing that I reported to her seemed unimportant—she would always listen with concentration, asking me to elaborate on some points.

I began a new program in the schoolroom with the younger students, one in which they would tell about things happening in their family. If they had news that nobody had heard before, I praised them and made them feel important.

If I was walking past two people in conversation, I would pause to pat an animal, pick a flower, fix a shoe, or otherwise delay moving on, in case I missed something useful to Grace.

Of a night, I would walk close to the cabins with my ears strained, hoping to pick up snatches of conversation.

The problem was that Gareth lived in a cabin that only contained three people: Leena, Isabella and himself. Isabella wasn't one of my students, so I couldn't get information from her.

Every night, straight after dinner and before going to help Mum, I would go to the shed and sit cross-legged on the grass, facing Gareth. Valerius rarely moved from his position on the bed or in the chair that was pulled up to a small desk near the doorway, and rarely disturbed us.

Gareth was reading the book about Ancient Rome and would relay the information to me in minute detail. This went on night after night and I sensed some over-excitement in this interest. It seemed a bit over the top.

One night he read me a paragraph about one of the ancient emperors, Titus. "Listen to this," he said. "*As a young man, Titus was dangerously like Nero in his charm, intellect, ruthlessness, extravagance and sexual desires. Gifted physically and intellectually, exceptionally strong, short with a pot-belly, with an authoritative, yet friendly manner and a supposedly excellent memory, he was an excellent rider and warrior. He could also sing, play the harp and compose music.*"

"Interesting guy."

"The Colosseum was completed during his reign. He was liked by the people. The thing is that he ruled for less than three years."

"Really? How come?"

"Died. Some say he was poisoned by his own brother who was next in line for Emperor."

"Not nice."

"It happened a lot back then. But I like this Titus guy. I'd like to be like him."

I laughed. "You'll have to tell everybody that you're to be known by the name Titus from now on."

I was joking. Gareth, however, seemed to find the idea attractive.

"Yeah. I've always hated my name. I could change it to Titus."

"I'm not sure that you can just change your name like that."

"Who's to stop me? The name police?"

"Very funny."

"I'll ask my mother. If she has no objection, I don't know why anybody else would."

Now that I was a companion to Grace, my time helping Will in his workshop was even more limited. I tried to keep to the roster as much as possible, but was sometimes delayed. Other times I would have to leave early.

Will liked to ask me about my new duties, about what I did for Grace and what she discussed with me. When Will visited Meg and William, Grace remained hidden. In this way, she became a puzzle that Will needed to solve. She became a woman of mystery. Will would quiz me about her personality, her intelligence, her motivations. He wanted to know about Valerius and what role he played in her life. These questions made me feel uncomfortable. My answers were stripped of detail and heavily censored.

I found it fascinating that Will didn't seek Valerius' company. I thought he would see the stranger as a fresh source of information. Will only visited the shed once, however, and that seemed enough to cure his curiosity. I know he found Valerius' presence frustrating, because it was delaying William's move to the community. Will was impatient for William's knowledge and advice about the projects he was working on.

So, in this manner, community life went on around Valerius, who was kept apart from it. Grace would visit her former lover rarely, always after dark so that her presence remained a secret in the community, and always with both eyes bandaged. She would only stay a matter of minutes before pleading ill-health and leaving.

One day I questioned her about Valerius' habit of staying in the shed. Wouldn't he be bored? Wouldn't he want to get out into the fresh air and walk around? Grace was shaking her head. "Many of the Elite are lazy. It comes from their sense of entitlement—there's always a brown-eye around to do whatever is needed. I was considered very different because I kept myself fit. Valerius' brother, the one who died in the fight, was also a bit different—he learned martial arts—but that was rare."

"Was the Emperor lazy as well?"

"Oh, yes, unless the activity had something to do with pleasure."

"It must be so…boring!"

"You're right, Melli. The Elite are their own worst enemy. Their health is already compromised by breeding habits, then they make it worse by lifestyle. Serves them right."

"What do you mean, serves them right?"

"I mean, things are going to end badly for them, but they deserve it."

My father was back at The Farm at Nambour and this time he had a sparkly-eye as a worker. India had convinced Dad that Isabella should have a turn at the satellite settlement, without mentioning a reason. Dad had complied, figuring that the girl would probably be the least problematic of Will's children—a good first test.

Normally Gareth would be jealous and upset about his sister going to The Farm before him, but guarding the stranger gave him a sense of importance. He wouldn't want anybody else taking over this duty. He barely mentioned the fact that Bella was going.

One night, when I went to check on Gareth and Valerius, I noticed that my friend was wearing overalls like mine. He normally favoured track pants that were comfortable for his pear-shaped body. This was quite a change.

"Hey, are you following my fashion trend? Where did you get the overalls?"

"There were some at the community store—thought I'd try them. They're great!"

"I like them when I'm teaching because they have so many pockets. I can whisk things out of sight without the little ones realising. Then there's this big pocket that I can put my notebook in, just in case I have time to write something."

"Yeah, well I like them because they've got that opening, inside, next to the normal pockets. You can reach through to stuff underneath."

"Like what?"

Gareth reddened. "You know…you want to scratch your belly, or adjust your jocks."

"I don't wear jocks."

"You know what I mean. If you're wearing shorts underneath and want to get something out the pocket…"

I lost interest in the subject and let it drop. Gareth wanted to talk more about the Roman Empire, but I had heard enough about it during our nightly discussions.

"Isn't it time you moved on to another stage in history?"

"Nah, I'm only halfway through the book. I reckon it's a shame that I'll probably never travel to Rome. I'd like to see the ruins—stand where Titus did, and walk in his footsteps."

"Yeah, I know what you mean. It wasn't long ago that

people did that, just caught a plane to Rome or Paris. Imagine." I sighed.

"Do you reckon we'll ever be able to do that—travel long distances?"

"I don't think so. Your Dad reckons the Northern Hemisphere is too messed up. Radiation."

"Yeah, that's what he tells me, too."

"We'll just have to dream about it."

"Or I could create my own version of Rome."

"What do you mean?"

"I could build a small Roman amphitheatre. Hold events there."

"Gosh, really? Where would you put it?"

"Past the solar panels and down on the side of the hill. I could excavate so that the seats were dug into the slope, terrace-like. Then have a flat area as a stage."

"So that would be just below the wind turbines."

"Yeah, I reckon the turbines look graceful when they move slowly, like a dance."

I laughed. "Sure. That would be a good spot. What sort of performances?"

"Plays and things. We could do some Shakespeare. Wrestling, too. Like they had in Rome.

"That's a terrific idea. You'd need help to build it."

"I reckon I could put together a crew—promise them roles in plays."

"Yes, I could see you doing that."

"Hey, we could go down there now. Have a look at the site."

"What for?"

"Just to have a look."

I frowned. "Way down past the solar panels?"

"Yeah. It would be fun."

Why did the air change when he made these suggestions? It made me shiver. "Nah, you'd better stay here and look after Valerius, and I have to get back to the cabin. It's bed time for the little ones."

"Whatever." Gareth turned his attention back to the book, the set of his shoulders betraying his disappointment. I got up and walked away.

A DAY AT THE FARM

Mum was looking at Dad with an expression of defeat. She had raised her arms and dropped them back to her sides. "I don't know, darling. I'd have to get all the children ready and then feed the babies. They'd be bumped and shaken all the way there. I'd have to arrange lunch for all the children at The Farm. Then they'd all get bumped and shaken on the way home."

Dad laughed. "It's meant to be a treat, not torture!"

Mum sat down and rubbed her forehead. "I'd love to go, darling, but it would be anything but a treat. It would be hard work."

Dad looked disappointed. He needed to do something

unusual—go to The Farm and back in one day. This was an opportunity to take the whole family so that we could all see where he worked. The problem was that Mum wasn't excited about the idea.

"Can anyone else look after the babies? That would give you a break."

Mum frowned. "Of course not. They have to be fed."

"How about if someone looked after some of the middle ones?"

"Maybe, but there's also the problem of this pregnancy. I don't think I want to be shaken up that much on the roads. Sorry, darling. It is a great idea and it would have been a nice break, but I don't think I can go."

Dad wasn't the only one disappointed by Mum's attitude. I hadn't seen The Farm for many years. I was longing to get away from the settlement. Mum must have sensed my disappointment.

"Take Melli. She's been working hard and deserves a break."

Dad looked at me. "Where are you meant to be working today?"

"In the schoolhouse until lunchtime, and then in the laboratory."

"Okay, I'll go and speak to Heather and Will. Hold tight."

I watched with affection as my father crossed the settlement. He was shorter than Mum, and described as 'stocky'. Actually, he was a powerhouse of energy. His compact body was strong and muscular, and I never saw him grow tired. He was a man people called on when a job just had to get done.

Like his father, George, Dad had a constant shadow of whiskers on his face, no matter how much he shaved. He also had a deep voice that resonated around any space he was in. If he ever broke into song, people would stop what they were doing to listen.

What I admired most about my father was his unwavering cheerfulness. His positive attitude and energy was a pleasant counterpoint to my mother's exhaustion. I missed Dad when he wasn't around.

It wasn't long until he returned, wearing a smile. "Okay, Melli-belly. Get dressed and grab your stuff. We're off to The Farm!"

He didn't need to say it twice. I was worried that someone would change their mind and I'd have to stay home. I was in my overalls and ready within minutes.

Over the years that The Farm had been operating, Dad had found that more and more roads had become impassable. He was always trying to find better routes.

What was once a drive of an hour or so, had become a tortuous journey of around three hours. Dad would navigate the treacherous road which led down the mountain, watching for washouts all the way. Sometimes he had to stop the vehicle and inspect the road before proceeding. Sometimes he would take a work crew and they'd have to do repairs.

As we made our way down the mountain on that fine day, I noticed the concentration on my father's face. He was unusually silent, and I noticed beads of perspiration on his forehead. We reached Landsborough with relief.

The main highway had deteriorated a great deal, but it was so wide that a safe passage could still be found. Dad could even drive at a reasonable speed along this stretch. When he got to the place where there was the ruin of The Big Pineapple—a tourist attraction—he would have to leave the highway and navigate another treacherous road which led to The Farm.

By the time we got there, I fully understood why Mum had declined the invitation. I'm sure the journey would have resulted in an early labour.

Once we passed through the main gates of The Farm, I allowed myself to relax and have a sense of excitement. There was a long driveway, but this was flat and kept in good condition. Dad, who had been silent most of the trip, except for the occasional expletive, now became talkative. He began telling me about the layout of The Farm and where the various crops could be found.

As we approached the dormitories, I saw a cloud of dust rising from the front of one of the doorways. It seemed like it didn't belong there so I looked for a cause. Then I saw something that made me gasp. Two boys were on the ground, punching and wrestling each other. They were so intent on this that they didn't hear the vehicle approaching. This sort of behaviour just didn't happen at Maleny, so I was becoming distressed. What would Dad do?

I was surprised to hear a chuckle coming from my father. He stopped the car and tooted the horn. The boys looked around and then leapt to their feet. They stood with heads bowed. Dad didn't say anything for a moment and I guess this was to keep the boys in suspense. Finally, he simply said, "Get back to work, lads." Their expressions showed surprise at first, and then relief. They fled back to the paddocks.

"I have to go and do the rounds of The Farm. Which would you prefer, helping Bella in the kitchen, or riding a horse with me?"

I could feel the broad smile on my face. "A horse? Wow! Yes, please."

"Okay. I'll get them saddled up. You can have old Stardust. She's quiet and obedient."

While Dad prepared the horses, I went into the house for a drink of water. Isabella was sitting in a chair in the kitchen, holding something that she would stroke every few seconds. I went over to have a look.

"Hi Bella. Oh, you have a kitten!" This was a particularly striking cat, black with white socks and a white tip on its tail. "Isn't it lovely."

Bella looked up and smiled. "Yeah, I've called it Sox."

"Is it a pet, then?"

"Yeah, Trent said I could keep it."

A flash of jealousy ran through me. At Maleny, pets weren't allowed. Every animal had a task or a purpose, otherwise they had to fend for themselves. Apparently the rules were different at The Farm or maybe just for sparkly-eyed Isabella. I wondered what would happen to the kitten when she returned home.

I noticed Isabella's happy demeanour. Farm life suited her. "How come Dad gave you kitchen duties? Don't you want to work in the fields with the others?"

"Yeah, but I was bugging Trent to make changes."

"What do you mean?"

"This farm isn't run on scientific principles. Anyone can see that. It was driving me crazy. I kept telling your father—"

"Ah, so he put you in here."

"Yeah, but that's okay. I can do what I like in here."

"I didn't know you could cook."

She laughed. "I can't! I try hard, though."

I smiled. This girl was totally different to the Isabella I knew back in Maleny. It was a big improvement.

I gulped down some water and looked out the window. Dad was leading the horses out. I tickled the kitten under its chin and told Isabella I had to go. "Take some biscuits," she said, opening a tin.

"Wow. Thanks. See you later."

"I guess you'll be here for lunch?"

"I suppose so."

"Great. I'll see you then."

I didn't realise how scary horses were, or how uncomfortable it was to ride them. First there was the height—I was afraid of falling. Then there was how wide my hips had to open. And the horse would keep moving around, even when we weren't going forward. I found the whole experience uncomfortable to say the least.

"You'll get used to it." Dad was seated comfortably on Admiral, who moved around a lot more than Stardust. "Just relax. Stardust will pick up on your tension otherwise. You'll be fine."

I took his advice and concentrated on relaxing. Soon we were moving towards the fields.

The first thing I noticed about The Farm was the different atmosphere. It was hotter than Maleny, and the light was harsher. I wished I'd brought a hat with me. I found the flies annoying as well.

Dad waved his hand over to the right. "The sugar cane and corn are for ethanol. This is a pain, because we have to grow so much for so little fuel. Will is working on the problem, but it's taking a while. It would be good if he could perfect the hydrogen cell technology."

"The Beast seems to be running alright."

"For short distances. I don't think it is reliable enough otherwise. Although he did say he'd give it a run down here soon." He brushed some flies away. "That's why I ride a horse here. I can't bear to use any more ethanol than I need to."

"The trip here and back today will use a lot of fuel."

Dad nodded. "But it was on Meg's orders. She needed some things that couldn't wait until my next trip."

And what Meg wants, Meg gets, I thought to myself.

We rode past the biggest dam, which boasted plenty of water. Dad nodded his head towards it. "The workers love to jump in there at the end of the day."

"Ew. It looks muddy."

"After a day working in this heat, muddy water isn't a problem."

"I guess not. Tell me about Bella. She said you got annoyed at her nagging."

Dad laughed. "Those kids of Will's—their brains are so advanced it's frightening. Imagine a thirteen-year-old girl quoting scientific farm data to me. I couldn't understand half the words, let alone their meaning."

"So you plonked her in the kitchen?"

"Yeah. And I have to give her credit for how hard she's trying. Also her attitude. When the others give her a hard time about her cooking, she laughs along with them."

"She looked happier than I've seen her for a while."

"I thought so, too. She's a good girl. Nice to have around, as long as she isn't nagging me."

Dad stopped to give orders to a group of workers. They were to pick some fruit and vegetables for Meg and bring them to the house. We rode on.

"I think some of this stuff is for William. Meg is trying to find the right diet for him."

"Ah, okay." My stomach began rumbling. I took some biscuits from my overalls' pocket and offered one to Dad. He looked at them and shook his head. I took a bite and realised why. They were awful. I ate them anyway.

"We can get some apples soon, and feed one to Stardust. She'll love that."

Our route had taken us to the northern end of The Farm, and we were now circling back towards the orchards. I could see the fruit, bright against the green leaves. Dad pointed. "We'll take some back with us, a few crates for the community to share."

As we passed the tanks that held drinking water, I saw a sight that surprised me. Marie, the environmentalist, and her twin brother, Peter, had a folding table set up in the shade and appeared to be conducting experiments. I didn't even know they were at The Farm. Dad and I rode over.

"Hi Trent," said Peter. He looked at me. "Hello, there." He obviously didn't know my name.

Dad replied. "Hi Peter. You know my daughter, Melisandre." I noticed something unusual in my father's voice. He was usually friendly and relaxed with everyone, even Meg. When he spoke to Peter, however, I could hear the lack of enthusiasm in his tone.

"Of course. Hi. Nice day for riding."

I smiled and nodded. Marie was bent over the table, preoccupied. She waved without looking around.

Dad nodded towards the tanks. "How's the water quality?"

"Good," said Marie with her head still bowed. "No problems here. We're going to check the septic systems next."

This news seemed to make Dad happy. "Great. How much longer are you staying here?"

"When are you going back?" asked Peter.

"This afternoon. Come along if you want."

"We might just do that. I'll let you know."

As we rode away, I considered Peter and Marie. I knew they were India's children, but wondered about their father. I asked Dad.

"A sad story. India's husband was an environmental scientist called John. He was killed in a snake attack. Those two, Peter and Marie were there when it happened, apparently."

"How old were they?"

"Only toddlers, I think. John saved the lives of many children, not just his own."

"That's sad." I thought for a moment. "So India must have been pregnant when it happened."

"Um…don't know. Don't think so."

"Well, Leena and Ruth—who would their father be otherwise?"

Dad frowned. "Yeah, good question. The timing doesn't

quite add up. It was before my time, though."

"I suppose so." The seams of my overalls were chafing along my inner thighs, where the saddle kept up constant pressure. I was hot and feeling sunburned. I didn't want to make a fuss, though. This was a special day. I stood in the stirrups and tried to re-arrange the legs of my overalls. Dad watched in amusement.

"Let's go and get something to eat," he said, much to my relief.

I have this thing in my mind that drives me crazy sometimes. It's when there is an unanswered question, or something that doesn't make sense.

Since talking to Dad about Leena and Ruth's parentage, the puzzle kept running through my mind. If their father wasn't John, then who was it? How many people could it be? I ran the names of the elders through my mind. Luke and George were the only two other men around at the time. I couldn't imagine Luke fathering children by India. George? More likely than Luke, but still…I couldn't imagine it, knowing the people involved.

As I chewed on the salad that Isabella had managed to prepare competently, I kept thinking about this. I had never heard the subject raised. It was a mystery. Even Dad didn't know the answer.

I heard a commotion outside, and then someone was

running into the house. It was George Junior, the second in command. He looked at Dad.

"Trent. There's been an accident."

Dad leapt to his feet and grabbed his hat. "What's happened?"

"It's Peter. The silly idiot slipped and fell into the septic pit."

"No!" A smile spread across Dad's face. He could see the humour in any situation.

"Actually, it's a bit serious. He banged his head on the way down. Became unconscious."

"So, he was in the pit, knocked-out?"

"Yeah. Robbie had to jump in and rescue him."

Dad groaned. "Oh, no. So has Peter come around?"

"Yeah, but groggy. Marie wants to get him back to Maleny for treatment."

I could tell Dad was annoyed. His nice, relaxed day at The Farm with me had just been hijacked by someone else's stupidity or carelessness. "Okay," he said with resignation. "We'll load up the car with Meg's stuff and some apples. Then we'll put Peter and his sister in the back. Marie can care for him while we're travelling."

"Okay. I'll get that underway."

Dad looked at me. "Sorry, Melli-moo. We'll have to head home in a few minutes."

That was okay by me. It beat climbing back on the damned horse.

The worst part about the long drive home wasn't that it was hot, or that there were constant bumps in the road. The worst part about the trip home was the smell. The septic pit contained human waste. Peter had fallen in. It wasn't pleasant.

We drove with all the windows wound down and the fan on full blast. We tried holding our noses. Nothing worked. Dad drove as quickly as possible, but it still took over two and a half hours to return home.

Along the way, I gently questioned Marie about her father's death. I asked how old she and Peter had been at the time. I then thought about how old Ruth and Leena were. The trouble was that Marie didn't know exactly how old they'd been when their father passed away.

Peter was groaning and thrashing around by the time we got back to Maleny. Marie took him straight to the clinic, with Dad's help, while I was sent to fetch India.

After that, I didn't know what to do. It wasn't even three o'clock. I ended up going to the laboratory to help Will.

A MYSTERY SOLVED

I was meeting Grace daily, but didn't have much to tell her. I tried very hard, lying awake every night trying to process each piece of information that had come my way during the day, just in case I'd missed something important. One morning I explained how I felt, that it was as though I was letting her down. She said she didn't feel that way at all. She knew I was trying. "I'm just waiting," she said. "Things will become obvious soon. You watch. We just need to be patient."

I told her about the mystery, the one about Ruth and Leena's father.

Grace's brow furrowed. "It wasn't John?"

"Dad said the timing didn't quite work, but he wasn't sure.

Maybe he is wrong."

"But we should be sure. We should be absolutely certain of this. It could be important. Who else could it be?"

When I explained that the only other two men around at the time were Luke and George, Grace shook her head. "That doesn't make sense. A mystery indeed. I'll look into this."

I was worried then, concerned that Dad was wrong and that I was sending Grace on a wild goose chase. I told her so.

"No, Melli. Everything is important. Any tiny piece of information you can bring will be appreciated whether it is right or wrong. I have time on my hands and am happy to look into anything you bring me. Experience has shown that if someone like your dad thinks something like that, then chances are it is right."

Another day I asked Grace if I could meet William, but she shook her head. "He is another person who might try to work against us when it becomes time to act. You'll meet him eventually, I promise. For now, I'd like to keep you and me separate from the others. It will work better."

I tried to hide my disappointment, but I think she could sense it. She looked at me with her good eye sparkling. "Hey, but I have something else for you."

I could tell this would be good. "What?"

"We have an answer to the mystery."

"What? The one about Leena and Ruth's father?"

Grace nodded.

"Well, who was it?"

"Do you know that nobody else in this community knows, other than William and now me?"

"So, William told you?"

"That's right. It's a huge secret."

I bit my lip. "But you'll tell me?"

"I couldn't not tell you. Not after all the help you've given me."

"Who was it?"

"Believe it or not, it was a man called Derek. A paediatrician."

I looked at Grace with a frown. "But…"

"Yes. I know. It's one of these time travel things. Very complicated."

"But India must know."

"You'd think so, but apparently not."

"Golly. What do we know about this Derek guy?"

"Not a great deal. Good man. Intelligent. Tall. Good looking."

"And what happened to him?"

"William was a bit vague. Something about sending him back in time to die with his wife and family."

"Oh…how sad."

"William seemed uncomfortable about the whole episode—seemed that Martin was the main person involved. He'd struck a deal with Derek and all of this was the result.

I shook my head. There was so much I didn't know. "This

time travel business—it's caused a lot of problems, hasn't it?"

"Yes, Melli. We must put an end to it. Very soon."

Then I witnessed something that confused me. After a busy day, split between Will's workshop and the schoolhouse, I spent a difficult few hours helping Mum feed the children and put them to bed. I felt resentful towards Zac, who always seemed to be absent during these times. Sometimes I'd mention this to him and his answers always infuriated me. "That's girls' work," he'd say and slouch off.

On this night I felt as though I'd been stretched too far. I knew Zac's day had been a fairly easy one, just helping Luke around the place, and this made my resentment worse. After the cabin had quietened for the evening, I told Mum I was going to find my twin and talk to him about it. She just sighed.

It was a beautiful evening. A new moon had risen from the east and looked splendid in the darkening sky. I stopped to listen to the various sounds floating through the air, trying to isolate my brother's voice.

I did one tour of the settlement without success. Where could he be? I widened the search by moving into the forest, towards the place where I used to sit and write.

A voice floated out, faint and indistinct. I wondered if my twin had taken a girl away from the settlement for privacy. I smiled. Busting him with a girl could be fun. I crept forward.

The next sound I heard was puzzling. It was the distinctive tone of Grace's voice. She spoke a sentence or two, and then somebody replied. Gareth.

I got close enough to see them. Grace's big bandage was in her hand—she must have been visiting Valerius. She was sitting next to Gareth on the log where he and I once sat. There was something about her attitude that alarmed me. She was leaning towards Gareth, looking into his eyes. Was she coming on to him?

I didn't wait to find out. I turned and walked out of the forest in a state of confusion. What was that about? How long had Grace been meeting Gareth? Why was she meeting him?

Common sense suggested that this was part of her plan, and that everything would become clear in due course. Maybe if I asked her she'd tell me. But why didn't she bring it up? Why didn't she trust me enough to tell me about meeting Gareth?

The thing was that I couldn't bring myself to ask her.

GOOD RIDDANCE

"That's good work Melli." Will was smiling as he inspected the records. "You've captured all the data perfectly. I wish the other helpers could do as well as you."

This is what I liked so much about Will. He was generous in his praise. It brought out the best in me.

It had been a long afternoon and I was feeling a lag in energy. Will poured us both a glass of water and brought mine over to where I was sitting. He pulled up a chair. I liked it when he did this. It meant we were about to have a friendly chat.

"You know," he said, "Things will be great when we finally get William here to help. He knows so much; we'll be able to perform miracles."

I wriggled in my chair. How good would that be? "I can't wait."

"Neither can I. It's taking so long."

"Stupid Valerius. I wish he'd never come."

"Hmm. He's certainly complicated everything."

"If only we could get rid of him."

Will nodded. "But we don't dare to interfere with him in case it causes some sort of change, here or in the future."

"I know, but couldn't we put him somewhere else? Why doesn't Meg send him to The Farm, for instance?"

Will was about to have a drink of water when I said this. The glass went back to the desk, forgotten. "Yes! Why didn't I think of that? We could send Gareth with him, which would help with another problem."

"What's that?"

Will looked at me, as though stuck for an answer. Eventually he said, "Oh, just behavioural problems. Maybe some manual farm work would be good for him."

"Yeah. He seems…I don't know…a bit obsessive about things."

"He hasn't been pestering you, has he?"

I didn't know how to answer—didn't want to be disloyal to Gareth, even if he had been creeping me out. "Oh, sort of. Yes, nothing I can't handle, though."

Will leapt to his feet. "That's it then. He goes, with or without Valerius. But with him is preferable." He stared out the window for a moment, then began removing his lab coat. "Do you know what? I'm going to see Meg right away. I'm going to get this sorted. Thanks for your idea, Melli. You're a great help."

The next day, I looked out the schoolhouse window to a scene that made me smile. Will had driven the Beast up to the shed where Valerius was staying. Gareth was already in the back seat and Will was ushering Valerius into the front. Doors banged shut and the Beast came to life. I waved goodbye, but only Will waved back.

As I walked around the community that evening, I noticed that there was a buzz in the air. People stood around in small groups, talking about the fact that Valerius and Gareth would be gone for at least a month. The mood at Maleny had lifted. It felt like a holiday atmosphere.

I picked up one of the toddlers, Annie, and roamed around with her, pulling faces and making her giggle. This was a ruse on my part—it looked like I was doing something, whereas in fact I was eavesdropping. I could see Heather and India in earnest conversation off to one side, so I scooted around the back of the hall to come out behind them. When I came within listening distance, I sat on the grass with my back to them and played with Annie.

Heather was talking earnestly. "…hope that he can handle Gareth."

India was quick to reply. "He's had a lot of experience with teenagers on The Farm. I wouldn't worry too much."

"But you heard about the ewe, didn't you?"

"Ewe? What ewe?"

Heather laughed, but it wasn't joyful. "I can't believe nobody told you. You know how he's been going around, playing with himself inside those overalls…"

"Yes. I'd heard about that, but…"

"George caught him with a ewe, carrying it into the forest, you know, like guiltily."

India didn't say anything for a few seconds. "What do you think he was going to do with it?"

"George and I both suspect either a ritual killing, like they did in Rome, or something sexual."

"No. Really?"

"Really. Maybe both. The boy is clearly oversexed. Everyone is talking about it."

India sighed. "So the idea was to send him to The Farm, toughen him up?"

"And watch over Valerius, who nobody seems to know what to do with."

"What a combination. At least everyone here seems happier tonight."

"They're excited because William might come and stay for the month. I got one of the girls to change the sheets on the bed, the one in the shed where Valerius slept. He can stay there."

India laughed. "That's where he stayed all those years ago when he first came here."

"Oh, really? I didn't know that. It will feel like home to him, then."

I heard somebody else approach, but didn't turn around. Grandpa George's voice boomed in the clear evening air. "Hello lovely ladies. Aren't you both a sight for sore eyes." I heard him give Heather a kiss. "How were things in the schoolhouse today?"

"Good. Nice. Gareth was busy packing for his trip, and then he left. It was a pleasant atmosphere."

"Hmm. I wonder how all of that will end up. At least we get a break from him. Hi Melli."

Damn. I'd been caught. I turned around. "Hi, Grandpa George. Hi Heather, India."

The women nodded. They must have been wondering how much I'd heard. I stood and brushed the grass from my overalls, then lifted Annie back into my arms. "Lovely evening!"

"Yes," the women said in unison. George nodded.

I walked on to the next group, trying to process what I'd just heard. Gareth 'played with himself' all the time? He did dirty things with ewes? I was slowly realising the extent of Gareth's problems, but it was just about to get worse.

THE TERRIBLE TRUTH

The sports shoes that Grace gave me made all the difference with my morning and evening ritual. I was running twice a day and feeling great. If I had to miss my exercise for any reason, the thrumming sensation returned very quickly, and I didn't like that.

Grace had explained, when she handed me the shoes, what caused that feeling. "It's sexual," she said, matter-of-factly. She shook her head when she saw me blush. "Nothing to be ashamed of. I had it myself."

"So all girls get it?"

"No. The only other person I've ever heard mention it is you—another thing we have in common. Exercise helps. Or you can pleasure yourself, which is a good idea."

"How do you mean?"

"If you calm that feeling every now and again, it makes you less susceptible to boys. A lot of girls end up pregnant because their desire overwhelms them."

"But…" I didn't know how to ask.

"Oh. You want to know how to do it?" Grace spoke for ten minutes or so, giving me instructions in her matter-of-fact manner. "Lick your fingers and start manipulating that little part of you between the folds of your vagina." As she described this act, I felt my groin region grow hot. I became slippery. My nipples tingled. I needed to do it right then and there. At the same time, I was embarrassed. I couldn't look her in the face.

"I've embarrassed you a great deal. I'm sorry, but it's something you need to know. Just find a quiet place and try it. At night, before you go to sleep is good. Or on a lazy morning."

"I don't have lazy mornings."

"Okay. In a bath. Whatever. Just try it and see if it helps. In the future, where I am from, there are all sorts of activities just related to sexual pleasure. VR, robotics—"

"What's VR?"

"Virtual reality. Anyway, that's only for adults, and Elite ones at that." She spoke on the subject for another few minutes until she could see my embarrassment easing.

That had been a few days earlier. Now my embarrassment

returned when I had to tell Grace about Heather and India's conversation. What Gareth was doing in his overalls, wasn't that what I'd been doing? Different action, same result? The whole idea of having to tell Grace mortified me. I blurted it all out, including my own feelings.

"Ah, I see. No, it isn't the same. The difference is that he does it constantly, apparently. Most boys and men masturbate, but in private. Many women do as well, but you'll never catch them. The thing is that Gareth seems to be at it all the time, and in public as well."

That made me more comfortable. I told her about the ewe. "Okay, now we know exactly what point we are at. That's excellent—thank you."

"What do you mean?"

"The big question in my mind was if Gareth's strange behaviour was partly caused by his mother's death and the awful circumstances causing it. Now we know that it wasn't a trigger. It happened regardless."

"So…"

"So, it is becoming clearer. There is little doubt that Gareth has severe problems that won't go away."

"What will you do?"

Grace stood and stretched. "Now that Valerius is at the farm, I'll start running again. How wonderful."

"Everybody," said Will proudly. "I would like to introduce to you my father, William."

By the time this introduction took place, the community was past impatience. Everyone had been waiting for weeks for William to arrive. The sight of the old time traveller caused a swell of excitement throughout the hall.

"There is someone else as well. William has a colleague called Aelia, who also travelled from the future. Don't get too attached to her, because she wants to return to her own time, if possible, whereas William would like to stay here with us."

"If everyone will have me," said the old man with a twinkle in his eye.

The crowd murmured their assent. Grace just nodded and didn't rise when Will introduced her. Clearly she wanted to fly under the radar.

Will continued. "I'm sure you'll make them both welcome. Please continue with your dinner and enjoy yourselves on this great occasion."

George had planned a special celebration in honour of William, and to a lesser extent, Grace. He had even carved an ice-sculpture, something never before seen in the community. The faces of the children, when they saw the carving of the koala, were priceless. Adults could see it wasn't very well done, but to the children, it was magic.

There were small cakes and other delicacies. Ice-cream, a special treat, was produced, and someone had even made a version of waffle cones. The hall buzzed.

Music began playing. Grandpa George had obviously selected the CDs because they were all by an old singer from long ago called Elvis Presley. I didn't like this music much.

Two tables had been placed together at the front of the room, reserved for the elders and time travellers. Will and Ruth were also seated there. Grandma Connie had arrived earlier, helped to her seat by Luke. I was at a table near the back of the room, to the right, sitting with my mother and siblings. From there I watched the interplay on the main tables, and in particular, Will's attention toward Grace. The two of them seemed oblivious to everyone else. They talked to each other like old friends, or two people with a great deal in common. It certainly did not appear as though they didn't know each other well. Ruth must have thought the same, because her mood appeared to change. She didn't look happy.

Leena arrived late. She looked dishevelled and her eyes appeared to twitch as she scanned the room. She seemed to be searching for a place to sit. I knew it would be hard for her, with Gareth and Isabella both at The Farm. Nobody else in the community wanted much to do with her. I was about to mention this to my mother, who I was sure would invite her to our table, but then I saw Leena turn quickly and leave. Nobody else seemed to notice her absence.

Time went by quickly. I was busy helping Mum feed the little ones. Zac tried to keep them amused so they didn't want to get up from the table and run around. It was after their bedtime, and I knew that their behaviour would soon escalate into overexcited tears and tantrums.

Our table was close to the door, and because of this, it was Zac and I who first heard a vehicle climbing up the driveway. We shot each other puzzled glances. "It sounds like the people-mover," said Zac. We both bounded out of our chairs and ran to the door to see what was going on.

We covered our eyes with our forearms as the headlights glared. When the lights were extinguished, I could make out my father's second-in-command, George Junior, behind the wheel, and Isabella in the passenger seat. George was first out of the vehicle. He ran around to open Isabella's door. She looked at us and then fled, not to her mother's dwelling but to the cabin that housed Will and Ruth. George Junior raised his brows at Zac and me, and asked where Meg was. Sensing trouble, I told him to wait and I'd get her.

I couldn't catch Meg's eye, however hard I tried. I'm sure everybody else in the hall saw my attempts. In the end I had to stand at her elbow and touch her lightly on the shoulder. She looked up. "Yes, what is it?"

"Um—there's somebody outside that needs to see you."

Meg frowned. "Somebody? Who?"

"George Junior," I said quietly. "I think there may have been trouble at The Farm, by the looks—"

Meg rose and pushed past me. I followed her. Will also began rising out of his seat, but seemed to change his mind. He was obviously enjoying Grace's conversation.

By the time I reached the door, George Junior was already giving his report. "…we don't know what happened."

"What do you mean?"

"Bella. She's really upset about something, but she won't tell us what."

Meg was frowning. "I don't understand. Start at the beginning."

"This afternoon. Troy couldn't find Gareth among the workers. He went back to the main buildings and found Bella crying. Wouldn't say why. Gareth was in the men's dormitory. Troy sent him back out to the fields."

"And Bella—do you have any theories?"

George Junior shook his head. "She was fine up until then. Really happy."

Meg sighed. "Where is Bella now?"

"I brought her back. She ran over there." He pointed to Will's cabin.

"And Gareth, he's still at the farm?"

"Yeah."

"Get something to eat from inside before you go back. We're having a celebration to welcome William."

"Can't. Have orders. Gotta go back right now."

Meg sighed. "Fine. Go then."

George Junior looked relieved to be dismissed. He leaped into the vehicle and took off at speed. Meg stood with her eyes closed for a few moments, and even in the dim light, I could see how slumped her shoulders were. She turned and began walking back into the hall. That's when she noticed me standing there. She looked as though she was about to say something, but changed her mind. After taking a few steps, she came back.

"Why is it, Melisandre, that every time there is a drama in this community, I turn around and find you standing just behind me?"

I raised my brows and shrugged. "I don't know."

"Well, I guess if you heard all of that, you may as well make yourself useful. Go and see if Bella is alright. I need to get back inside. I don't want anybody to know there is a problem." Straightening her shoulders, she walked back into the hall and re-joined the celebrations as though nothing were wrong.

As I crossed the grassed area to Will and Ruth's cabin, I had a sense of unease, but couldn't quite work out what was causing it.

The cabin was dark. At first I thought that Isabella had gone somewhere else, but then I heard a snuffling sound. I followed it into the main bedroom. The girl was sitting on the floor with her back to the wall. Her head was lowered onto her forearm, which rested on her knees. Her shoulders were heaving.

I took in the scene for a moment, not knowing what to do next. I went over and stood, looking down at her. She didn't raise her head. I lowered myself to the floor and rested my back against the wall beside her.

"Hey, are you okay?" I asked softly. I put my hand on Bella's arm, but she shrugged it off. There was no answer. I ploughed on. "Meg told me to come over here and see how you were. You don't have to say anything. I'll just sit here."

I crossed my legs and looked around the room. There was a faint light shining through the window from the community hall. I could hear the murmur of voices and occasional laughter. I saw a spider caught in a web under the bed. Boredom was setting in and I was missing the celebrations. My mother would need me soon to help put the little ones to bed.

I decided to try another tack. "Gareth…he's not my friend anymore. He's been doing stuff that makes me feel uncomfortable. So if you need to talk to someone, you can trust me."

Bella's head was still buried in her knees, so her voice was muffled. "What did he do to you?"

"He's been getting over-friendly with me—trying to get me to go off with him, just the two of us. One day he tried to grab me—my breast, and kiss me. It felt weird, so I've been avoiding him."

Bella lifted her head then, and I was shocked by what showed on her face. All the fresh innocence was gone. She looked older, and even the special, sparkly eyes looked flat. "He's mad," she said dully. "My brother is crazy. I hate him.

My mother too. They're both mad."

"What has he done? What did he do to you?"

Bella didn't say anything for a few minutes. When she started talking, the words began slowly, quietly. I had to strain to hear her at first. "I was in the main house—on kitchen duty. I was at the sink, starting early preparations for dinner. All the others were in the fields, except Valerius who was over at the men's dormitory. I was bending down to get a colander out of the cupboard when I felt hands on my waist. I spun around. Gareth was there and he had a weird look on his face, like…like a leering mask. I asked him what he was doing there but he didn't answer. He unclipped the straps of his overalls so they fell down to his ankles. His… you know…his thing…it was bulging."

Bella's voice was getting louder and the words came faster. "I was too slow. I didn't think this sort of thing was possible, that a brother would come on to his sister—twin sister—like that. I can't remember what I said to him, but it was something to get rid of him. I wasn't taking the whole thing seriously." She stopped talking for a few minutes and her breath came in shudders.

"Then he grabbed my wrists, really hard. It hurt. I tried to twist my way out of his grasp, and got sort of free, but he grabbed my hair. I realised then that I was in trouble. He pushed me hard, and I fell to the floor. My head hit something. I don't think I blacked out, but I was sort of out of it. Dazed. Then I realised he'd pulled up my dress and was struggling with my underpants. I started to buck my whole body, but he seemed to like that."

I wanted to stop her then—tell her I didn't need so much detail. It felt weird that she was telling me everything. I figured that the worst was yet to come and had the urge to cover my ears. But it seemed as though she had to tell it all, that once she started she couldn't stop. Maybe she wanted to get rid of the poison, and thought that telling the whole story could purge herself of it.

"I screamed. He put his hand over my mouth and nose, so it was hard to breathe. I bit his hand, really hard until he took it away and I began screaming again. I felt a pain, between my legs. He was trying to force his way inside me. He was saying something over and over. "I am Titus. Call me Titus." Her words were coming faster, now, and her breath was ragged.

"He had his hand over my mouth again. I hated that. It felt like I was suffocating, that I'd die from lack of air. I was getting dizzy. His other hand was holding both of my wrists, above my head. I got one arm free and punched him in the temple. That stopped him for a second, enough time for me to bring one of my knees up. I kneed him, hard. Between the legs. He rolled off me, doubled over."

Bella's eyes were glazed and fixed as she relived the attack. "I got to my knees and reached up to the knife block. The big chef's knife was there. I lifted Gareth's head up by the hair and held the knife to his eye. I told him that I wanted to kill him. That he was mad. I said I never wanted to see him again. If he came near me, I'd stab him. He got up and ran away."

I could feel that the blood had drained from my head. I caught sight of my reflection on the window. My eyes were huge. "What happened next?"

"Everything went quiet. My head was aching where I'd banged it, and there was a burning feeling between my legs. I guess I sort of just curled up in a ball on the floor. After a while your dad came looking for Gareth. He found me like that."

"But you didn't tell him what happened?"

"How could I tell him? I felt…dirty…he's my brother. You can't tell anyone either." Her eyes grew fearful. "Promise?"

I hesitated. Someone should be told. Someone had to be warned about how bad Gareth had become.

Isabella turned and grabbed me by the shoulders. "Promise me you won't tell anyone. Please?"

I looked at her desperate face. "Okay. I promise," I said, but she couldn't see that my fingers were crossed.

We sat there in silence, the terrible truth filling the room with its thick poison. I put my arm around Isabella and she rested her head on my shoulder. I felt a sense of relief— lucky that I had trusted my instincts. This could have been me, and I may not have been able to fight him off.

Bella began talking again, this time in a dull monotone. The story wasn't quite finished. "After I'd packed and we were walking towards the people mover, I saw something hanging from the tank-stand, moving in the wind. I…I…" She was struggling to form the words.

I didn't understand. "What was it?" Isabella didn't answer. I had a thought and it sent chills through my blood. No. Surely not. "Not the kitten? Not Sox?"

Bella nodded and began making wailing sounds. I had no idea what to do. I just sat there, rocking her until she quietened.

There was a sound at the door. Ruth came into the room and surveyed the scene. She looked at us with a frown. "Meg said there is something wrong." We remained silent. "What is it?" Bella shook her head. "Do you know, Melli?"

I looked at Ruth for a moment and said, "No. I don't know what's wrong."

Ruth looked at Bella and held her arms open. The girl stood and allowed herself to be taken into her auntie's embrace.

Ruth looked over Isabella's head and caught my eye. Her eyes darted to the door. I took the hint and left the two of them alone.

TELLING GRACE

The following morning, I was able to go running with Grace, who was staying in one of the community caravans. We jogged to the end of the driveway and turned left, knowing that the views would be glorious on this fresh, Spring day. I tried my best to keep up with the speed of my friend, and noticed she would slow from time to time. In that way we managed to keep pace with each other.

We took a break at a rotunda that overlooked the mountains. This building often fell into disrepair, but George or one of his sons would always come and fix it, especially if there was a wedding planned. Luke and Connie had been the first to hold their wedding ceremony there, and that had started a tradition.

On this morning, it was the perfect place to sit and gaze into the distance. I sat on the wooden seat and wriggled until it felt comfortable. Then I turned to Grace. "I've got something to tell you, but wanted to get away from the settlement first. It's a secret."

Grace looked puzzled. "What?"

"Gareth tried to sexually assault his sister, Bella. At The Farm."

Grace nodded as though she'd been expecting this news. "Is his sister alright?"

"In a bit of a state. Doesn't want anything to do with her mother, either. I sat and talked to her for a while last night, until Ruth came into the cabin. Meg sent her."

"So that's why Ruth left suddenly."

"Bella swore me to secrecy, but I had to tell you."

"She will tell someone else eventually."

"Really?"

"Yes. For sure."

"I feel that someone needs to know, soon. Gareth is getting too dangerous. I don't think we can wait until Bella opens up. What can I do?"

Grace was silent for a moment. "Hmm. This is what I'd do. Wait until Isabella is back in the schoolroom and then tell Heather that you're sure something is seriously wrong with the girl. Say you think something terrible must have happened. Heather will see the state Bella is in and question her. Heather's had a lot of experience with teenagers, so will know how to draw it out."

"What if Bella won't tell her?"

"I think she will. Then Heather will tell the elders. They will go to Meg and tell her."

"What will Meg do?"

"That I don't know for sure. We'll have to wait to find out."

"What does Meg say to you now about Gareth? You know her better than I do."

Grace snorted. "No I don't. Just because I was living in her house doesn't mean she's been friendly."

"I guess she has a lot of worries, with the community and all that."

"She never liked having me there. Said I was useless. Mind you, she found William annoying as well."

I laughed. I couldn't think of anybody less useless than Grace. She was a very capable person. I told her so.

She smiled. "Meg was talking about housekeeping. I guess she had a point."

"How do you mean?"

"I was raised by a wealthy Elite couple. They had many servants. When I moved in to a place of my own, I took a servant with me."

"So you didn't learn about cooking or cleaning?"

"Exactly. Or laundry. All that was done for the Elite."

"How cool would that be?"

"Yes, but then when I was with Meg, I didn't quite understand how much work was involved in having William and me there. And Martin in the beginning."

"And India at one stage."

"Exactly."

"And Meg isn't young."

"I tried to help, but Meg called me useless. Said it was quicker to do it herself."

"That sounds like Meg."

"I think Will is almost ready to take over being leader. He is more charismatic and suited to the role."

"I noticed he enjoyed your company last night."

Grace flushed. "Yes. We got on well. He is—how can I say it—an engaging person?"

"Yes, I know. I feel that as well."

"I don't think his wife appreciated the attention he paid me."

"I noticed that too."

"Was it that obvious? How awful. In front of the whole community. I should leave Maleny as soon as possible."

"So, what I don't understand—you don't have the device to go back to your time, right?"

"Right."

"But Valerius does?"

"He says he has. William and I have searched the shed but can't find it. Either he has secreted it somewhere, or he took it to The Farm."

"But he has a thing for you, wants to marry you, so why don't you just ask him for it?"

Grace laughed. "You think I haven't tried that? I suggested that maybe it would be safer with me. He said no, and gave the excuse that a woman with two damaged eyes couldn't possibly keep it secure."

"Okay, something else I don't understand. It was decided that Valerius and Gareth were to go to the farm. Valerius seemed to go without argument, which seemed strange."

"True, and I have a theory about that."

"What is it?"

"I think he wanted to observe Gareth more closely, away from the prying eyes of the elders."

"Why?"

"Because he's beginning to put two and two together."

"You mean he's seeing how Gareth caused problems in your time?"

"Yes, but he hasn't spoken to me about it yet. I expect him to when he comes back. Then I'll know more." She stood and placed a foot on the bench, stretching her hamstring. "Hey, I spoke to Will and William about a light aircraft. They're excited." She began swivelling her torso, and then stopped and smiled. "You might get to fly after all."

I could feel my face beaming. To soar through the skies was my greatest wish. Would it really come true one day?

Despite the problems which lurked below the surface, most things at Maleny remained unchanged. For more than a week following the celebratory dinner, life went on in the normal way with rhythms uninterrupted. Bella eventually emerged from her father's house with dark circles shadowing her eyes. She avoided Leena, who rarely left her own cabin.

If Will was worried about his daughter, he didn't mention it much, only saying that Ruth had suggested that the girl return to her lessons at school as soon as possible. Whatever ailed her might be fixed by going back to old routines.

William had begun helping his son in the workshop, which meant I finally got to meet the old time traveller properly. I enjoyed his courtly manners and deliberate way of talking. The way his eyes crinkled when he found something amusing was attractive to me.

Any time he spent at the workshop was busy, so I didn't have an opportunity to ask him any of the list of questions I would have liked answered. I knew that Grace didn't want me to have a lot to do with William, so I felt constrained. This was frustrating.

When old William wasn't in the workshop, my time with Will consisted mostly of answering questions about Grace. He admired the way in which she strove for what she believed in, whether it be physical fitness or changing an unjust world. He commented on the excellence of her brain. I could tell that he wanted to get to know her better. He wanted this quite badly.

One day he invited Grace to the workshop to help him and William with projects. She arrived and had a tour of the various projects, but wouldn't stay any longer. I was there at the time, and sensed her unease.

All through this time, I felt as though I was sitting on a time-bomb. I knew without a doubt that when everyone found out what Gareth did to Isabella the whole community would erupt into chaos.

THE WORD IS SPREAD

It was the first day of Isabella's return to school. She arrived a few minutes late, and made her way quickly to the special area where Will's children sat. Jack and Evie were already there, and shuffled their chairs to accommodate hers. Gareth's empty seat was pushed against the wall.

Bella's face betrayed the shock and suffering that she was clearly still experiencing. I noticed Heather watching her with a worried expression. When we stopped for a break, and the pupils had run outside, I took the opportunity to speak to my grandmother.

"Bella—there seems something badly wrong, doesn't there?"

Heather nodded. "I wish we knew what it was."

"It must be serious. She looks like death."

"What do you know about it—what have you been told?"

I chose my words carefully. "Only that it had something to do with Gareth. You know, I had problems with him— trying to seduce me all the time. Heavens knows what might have happened."

My grandmother began biting the inside of her mouth, a habit that only presented itself when she was deep in thought. She reached for her tea and took a sip. "Was she hurt at all—any physical injuries?"

"Not that I know of."

"Hmm. Do me a favour, would you Melli? Send her in here, but keep the other children outside for a while."

"Sure." I drained my glass of water and stood up slowly. I didn't want to appear over-eager, even though every instinct told me to run to the door before Heather changed her mind.

Bella was sitting on a bench, biting her cuticles. When I told her that Heather wanted to see her, she frowned. "Why. Did you tell her something?"

"Nope. I swear. Cross my heart."

Her eyes narrowed as she looked into my face. "You're sure?"

I looked back at her with attitude. "What do you take me for? I promised I wouldn't tell anybody and I haven't."

Bella sighed and nodded. "Okay then, I'll go in and talk to her."

My stomach squeezed in anticipation.

The children, sensing there was something in the air, began getting boisterous. They ran around the settlement, making noises that caused adults to peer out of buildings to see what was going on. I had to think of something quickly.

"Who wants me to read one of my stories out loud?"

There was a general chorus of approval. "Okay, all of you go and sit under the big fig tree. Arthur, grab me a chair out of the hall, would you?" I reached into the bib of my overalls and pulled out the notebook.

I positioned the chair so that I was facing the schoolhouse. The children were all looking at me, so were oblivious to anything happening behind them. I began reading the first chapter of the Boo-gang story, infusing it with a scary voice and evil face. I had them all in the palm of my hand.

Halfway through chapter three, I saw Heather open the schoolhouse door and hurry to the site where George was building a new cabin. I saw her talk to him, gesticulating. George threw his hammer on the ground and the two of them made their way quickly to the yard where the sheep were kept. I lost sight of them for a few minutes. Next, I saw George, Heather and Luke moving swiftly to Luke and Connie's cabin. The door closed behind them and everything went silent for five or so minutes.

Heather emerged first, and made her way over to me.

I stopped reading and smiled when the children groaned in disappointment. I held my finger to my lips and they quietened.

My grandmother smiled. "You've done a great job, sweetheart. Now I need to ask more of you. Move the children back inside, would you? Continue the lessons for the little ones. Get the older kids to help."

"Sure. Where are you going?"

"To see Meg. With George, Connie and Luke. I hope we won't be long."

I finished reading the chapter and promised them another one at the end of the day if they all behaved well. They moved into the schoolhouse in an orderly fashion. Isabella was sitting at the desk, red-eyed. I touched her on the shoulder and she gave me a half-smile.

Time dragged. I could almost hear every second of the clock ticking in my head. We broke for lunch, but I felt like I didn't have much appetite.

The four elders returned. Luke went into Will's workshop. Soon, Will could be seen driving out in the Beast. I saw the four elders standing in the sunshine, talking and gesticulating. Connie staggered slightly and took Luke's arm. A few more words were said before the meeting broke up. Luke walked Connie back to their cabin, one small step at a time.

Heather came back to me with smile. "You've done great, Melli. It's all over now."

"What happened?"

"Oh, nothing much—just to do with Gareth. You don't need to worry your pretty head about it. I'll just grab something to eat and we'll get these kids back in for the afternoon lessons. Okay?"

"Sure," I said with a smile.

But I wasn't smiling for long.

A SACRIFICIAL LAMB

It was the next day that I began to feel uneasy. Something was in the air. My father returned on schedule for the change-over of workers, but before he could see my mother, he was whisked away to meet with Meg. When he returned, his face was grim. He went into our cabin, shooed all the children out and said he needed to talk to our mother. The door was closed in our faces. Darkness fell and I took my younger siblings into the common room for dinner. They were misbehaving because they could sense the tension of the adults.

I delayed our return to the cabin for as long as possible, but the younger ones were overdue for bed. I knocked on the door and called out to Mum. The door opened and I checked my parents' faces for clues. What was going on? The next hour was taken up with baths, pyjamas and bedtime stories. The cabin calmed into quietness.

As I was putting books back on the shelf, I could feel Mum and Dad's eyes on me. I turned and folded my arms. "I've had enough of this. Are you two going to tell me what's going on?"

Mum nodded and pointed to the table and chairs in the kitchen. It was the only sitting area of the tiny cabin, but could be closed off from the bedroom area. Dad did this now, pulling the sliding door across and making sure it sat flush with the door frame.

Mum looked at Dad with what could only be described as disgust. This came as a shock to me. Normally her expression when she looked at my father was loving. This was highly unusual behaviour from her. "You tell her," she said to Dad.

This made my stomach twist. "What is it Dad? What is so terrible? Why isn't Zac here too?"

Dad sighed. "Because it doesn't concern Zac, but it concerns you. Meg has made a decision. She has given me instructions. It is to do with Gareth."

There was another twist to my stomach. "What? What are they going to do with him?"

"You'll never guess."

"Come on Dad. Tell me."

Dad looked at my mother and she raised her eyebrows at

him. Finally, he came to the point. "You're to marry him—become his wife."

The shock of this made me feel faint. I certainly hadn't seen it coming. Jeez, I thought they might have sent Gareth away, or flogged him or something. Not this. I raised my hands and waved them in protest. "No. No way."

"You know the rules, Melli-moo. Meg is our leader. She told me it is to happen as soon as Gareth comes back from the farm."

"Dad, tell me you didn't agree with this!" My voice had a begging tone. Dad lowered his eyes to the table. "Mum, tell me I don't have to do it."

Mum sat back in the chair, holding her swollen belly. "Your father says it's done. He has agreed. It is for the good of the community."

I stood suddenly, sending the chair crashing to the floor behind me. "For the good of the community?" I was aware of the pitch of my voice, high and weird. "You're worried about the good of the community? You have got to be joking!" My chest was heaving. "Mum, we've spoken about this. I thought I had choices in my life, could take my time."

Mum's face was pale and her lips thin. "I know, Honeybee. I thought you did have choices. Apparently that was a fantasy." She glared at my father. "Those choices have been taken away."

I spun around until I was looking squarely at my father. "You of all people—you know what he's like. He tried to rape his own sister! And now you've agreed that I'm to marry him?" My father continued to gaze at the floor.

I stared at my parents with mounting distress. This was beginning to feel like a nightmare. Perhaps I'd wake up and find that none of this really happened. My mouth opened and closed a few times but no words came out. I lurched for the door and slammed it behind me.

The door to Grace's caravan was closed, but she quickly opened it when she realised it was me banging on it with an open palm.

"Melli? What is it? What's happened? Have they harmed Gareth?"

I was sobbing so hard the words wouldn't come out. I shook my head and tried to catch my breath. Grace came toward me and held out her arms. "Here, here," she said. She held me tightly with one arm and stroked my hair with the other. "Come and sit down. I'll get you some water."

"They're going to make me marry him!"

"Who? What! Not Gareth!"

I nodded, still gulping. "I've been betrayed. By my own father!"

"Hush now. Settle down. Tell me the story from the beginning."

I watched Grace's face as I told the story. I saw the anger cross her features. When I was finished she nodded. "It's because he's so bloody precious, our Gareth. Grandson to Meg and William. And India, but that's of less importance. Son of Will. Gareth is oversexed so he needs a wife to settle him down." Grace shook her head. "You are the sacrificial lamb. I wonder what Meg did to coerce your father into agreeing?"

I had calmed down, but could still feel the tears running down my face, fat and hot. "I don't know. She just issues orders and he obeys. That's the way it has always worked."

"Your mother—"

"She said I had choices! She was the one that made me see that!"

"I bet she's very unhappy about this, Melli."

I nodded. "She is."

Grace stood and began pacing the tiny floor space of the caravan. "It can't happen, Melli. It must be stopped."

I looked at her with hope. "How?"

"See that bunk? You can sleep there tonight. I'll let your parents know you're here. Let me talk to them, okay?"

Grace left the caravan quickly. As soon as the door closed, I threw myself onto the bunk. Despite the turmoil in my mind, I fell into an exhausted sleep which featured weird dreams. If Grace came back that night, I didn't hear it. When I woke, it was to find that I was alone in the van.

TO WED OR NOT TO WED

I heard footsteps approaching the caravan and this made me stop writing and close my notebook. I hadn't been writing seriously, anyway, just words tumbling out about my feelings, which were confused. I hadn't left the caravan since the previous evening and was grateful for the privacy it offered. It sounded like this was about to end.

The knocking was harsh and loud. When I opened the door it was to the sight of Will, whose sparkly eyes were filled with sadness. "Can I come in? I need to talk."

"Sure, but Grace isn't here."

Will had to almost bend in half to enter the van.

"Yeah, I know. That's why I'm here. One of the reasons

at least. The other is that Meg wants to see you."

My stomach squeezed. "Well, I don't want to see her."

"Can't say I blame you. But I have to fill you in, anyway. Some bad stuff has happened. Meg will just have to wait until you and I have had a chance to talk."

There was something in Will's tone I hadn't heard before. Defiance. Anger, maybe. "Okay, sit."

Will folded his long frame into the seat that ran behind the fixed table. He cleared his throat. "I'm afraid I have some bad news."

Could it be any worse news than Gareth's and my impending marriage? "Oh? Go on."

"Meg and Grace had an argument this morning. A bad one. Shouting even."

"What about?"

"Gareth. After that it was about you and Gareth. Grace was adamant that Meg change her mind about the marriage. Meg told her to mind her own business."

"Gosh!"

"Grace said it *was* her business. There were things in the future, where she came from, that were caused by Gareth and she had to change them now. It escalated from there."

"Were you there?"

"No. Anyway, it gets worse…"

"How do you mean?""

"Not only didn't Grace change my mother's mind, but Grace was expelled from the community."

I felt a sense of rising horror. Poor Grace. How could a person survive without the support of the rest of us? "So where is she now?"

"I don't know. This happened at my mother's house. Grace left there and hasn't been seen since."

I had to find her. Straight away. I reached for my shoes. While I was lacing them up, I said, "It sounds like you're on my side. You don't want to see Gareth and me married?"

"No, and for all sorts of reasons. I don't know what Mum was thinking."

"What about William? What has he said?"

"Nothing yet. He doesn't know. You're the first to be told."

"Why me?"

"Because I knew you'd want to find Grace, and if you find her, then so will I."

My hands stopped mid-tie. "Why? Why do you need to find her?"

Will looked at me for a few seconds. "Because I must."

"Because you're afraid of how she'll cope on her own? Because you need her for a project? Because…?"

"Because I must." He stood. "C'mon. We'll take the Beast. We'll find her."

While Will and I were scouring the surrounding area for Grace, and not succeeding, two things occurred to me. One was that Grace was a natural runner and could already be a great distance from the settlement. The second contradicted the first—maybe Grace hadn't gone far, but didn't want to be found just yet.

After an hour of searching, Will and I drove into Meg's driveway. My stomach was clenching and unclenching like a fist and I felt a tremor in my hands. My breathing was shallow. I had never had a one-on-one interview with Meg in my life. I turned to Will. "Are you coming in with me?"

Will shook his head, but then looked into my eyes. "Hmm. Maybe I will. I think you want me to."

I could feel hot tears rising. I nodded.

"Well, okay. She may send me away, though."

I smiled grimly and we made our way to Meg's front door. Will entered without knocking, which I guess was okay because of the mother/son thing. Meg was sitting at a bench in the kitchen, on a stool, writing in a book.

"You took your time!" she said, glaring at Will.

Will didn't cower or explain, he just shrugged his shoulders. My hero.

Meg slid from her stool and came toward me, holding out her hand. "Melisandre. Thank you for coming. I think we are overdue for a talk. Let's go somewhere comfy, alright?"

Will wasn't included in this invitation, but followed nevertheless. When we reached the living room, Meg waved me inside then turned and shut the double doors firmly in Will's face. I half expected him to enter nonetheless, through another doorway, perhaps, but he didn't re-appear.

I looked around the room. One wall was all glass, with a view to the Glasshouse Mountains. On this particular day, the breeze was coming from the southeast—from the sea— and this caused the mountains to have a soft appearance. As views went, this was a special one.

I turned and looked around the rest of the room. Two whiteboards sat on easels, leaning against a wall. I crossed the room to look at them.

Someone had created a chart on the first board. There were items on the left, and check boxes on the right. The items were: Food, Clean Water, Shelter, Health, Clothing, Energy, Environmental Impact, Safe future for humans.

I was aware that Meg was standing near the window, watching my movements. I moved to the second board. This contained details of every person in the settlement by means of family trees. This was done neatly, all the letters carefully printed so as to be even. On the left were Luke and Connie, Heather and George's lines, while on the right there were India, Meg and William's.

I realised Meg had come to stand beside me. "We need to keep track of everyone," she said. "I also record all the details in journals, but sometimes I just need a quick reference."

I frowned. "When you look at it like this, you realise that the families on the left never breed with those on the right."

"And that's not a good thing. Fortunately, you are going to help us fix this."

Meg sat down on a sofa and waved me into the seat next to her. She took my hand, patting it as she smiled at me. "I think we've gotten off to a bad start, Melli. Sorry about that. I'd like you and I to be friends. Is that okay?"

A voice in my head shrieked, "Friends? You've got to be kidding!", but I nodded. I'd just play this out and see where it led.

"Good girl. I'd like to share some things with you, Melli. I'd like to tell you about 2013, and how things were in my life before it happened." I felt a surge of excitement. This would be interesting. "I had been married, but that failed and I was responsible for raising two children. My husband left me for a girl at the office." This was said flatly. "I found an excellent position as Executive Assistant to a business woman, who had confidence in my abilities despite limited credentials. I was extremely lucky. She changed my life—maybe even saved it." Meg paused for breath.

I felt uncomfortable with Meg holding my hand. I shifted slightly on the sofa, and Meg moved as well. She dropped my hand. "I became involved with a man who wasn't very nice and became pregnant to him. The birth was a nightmare. The child died. That happened on the evening of the thirteenth of May, 2013. When I woke from my chemically induced unconsciousness, it was to a world where everybody had died."

"Scary. But there were others still alive, though."

"Not in Victoria, where I lived. After a period of denial and rather terrible things, I drove up here to Maleny. It was a journey of almost two thousand kilometres, with many hazards. I was alone for a while and found this place. Then Luke found me and then both of us found Connie. Much later, Heather, George, India and John turned up."

"So that was it then, all the survivors?"

"No, there were two brothers who tried to keep India captive. Long story. William had turned up by then, and he dealt with the situation."

"How?"

"These guys were idiots to the point of subnormal. William thought it was better to destroy them than have them breed."

"Destroy them? How do you mean?"

"He had a weapon. Turned them into tiny piles of ashes."

"Do you mean he took their lives?" This was a weird concept for me—for anybody in our community. The thought of taking a precious life, well it just wasn't something that anyone would ever consider. We were there to create life, not destroy it. I didn't understand how William could have taken two lives.

"Yes, and since those early days I've tried my best for this community. I've done my utmost to make sure we survived. Well, not only survive, but thrive. Can you imagine a universe without human beings?" I shook my head. "Well, it came close, Melli. Several times. I'm amazed we're all still here."

I couldn't think of anything to say. I just nodded.

"What you should also know is that the world, before the pandemic, was seriously messed up."

"How?"

"So many ways. Terrorism, racism, domestic violence, wars, murder…. and we were killing our planet with pollution. Sheer stupidity. This community is humankind's chance to start afresh. That's why I insist we lead sustainable lives and that there is no greed or violence."

I thought about the two boys that I saw fighting at the farm and wondered what Meg would have done with them had she witnessed that scene.

Meg kept talking. "William told me that the only original survivors were Luke and Connie—so young! In the future, the population was suffering because of what those two went through. William and Martin travelled back in time on several occasions, inoculating people against the virus, so there would be more survivors to help the young couple. That's how I survived. My role was to help the young ones. Later they inoculated the others as well. There should have been more, but the whole time-travel thing became a problem."

"So you lost the two children you had to your husband, plus another baby?"

"Yes. My parents as well. We all lost the ones we loved. It was an awful time."

"Yeah. I see that."

Meg stood and began moving around the living room, touching items as she went. "I know I have a reputation, Melli, of being a tough old bitch." She turned and looked at me. I shrugged. "Well, I guess I've earned that, because it has been hard. Every good thing in this new world has come at a cost. Survival has been difficult. Those like you who were born in the past fifteen or twenty years have no idea."

"I suppose so."

"Everything I've done, every action since 2013 has been for the good of the community. I've had to be strict and firm. I try to be fair."

I frowned at her then. Fair? Forcing me to marry her over-sexed grandson? That wasn't fair at all.

Meg continued. "I guess you don't think it's fair that you have to marry Gareth, but I can't see another solution, can you? Should we lock him up? Expel him? Everybody tells me you are an exceptional person, Melli. Tell me an alternative."

Meg was asking me an adult question. I wanted to give her an adult answer. The problem was that I was ill-equipped to do so. I sat there, dumbly, with a blank mind. Finally, I shook my head in defeat.

Meg nodded. "You see, it isn't easy. This community needs all the people we have, and more. And we need them all to breed."

Emotions that were beyond my control welled up and spilled out. "I'm too young to have babies!"

"I was told you'd started menstruating."

"Yes, but—"

"But nothing. Menstruation is the sign that you're ready to bear children. Every time you bleed is because your egg hasn't been fertilised."

"But you only had one baby in this settlement!"

Meg nodded. "Yes, that makes me look hypocritical, doesn't it?" I nodded. "There were compelling medical reasons for that, however. My three previous confinements had been train wrecks. I was needed here to help Luke and Connie, not die in childbirth."

"What about Peter and Marie?" I recalled the last time I saw this strange brother and sister. Peter had been covered in human excrement and delirious, while Marie was trying to nurse him. I fought down an urge to laugh. "They've never married, never bred. How come they get away with it?"

"Good question. This was raised last week, as a matter of fact. Peter is planning on selecting a wife very soon, probably in twelve months or so. Marie—well—she's running out of time. I've told her to pick someone now."

"It's hard to imagine them with anyone. They seem so… sexless."

Meg looked at me with an odd expression. "That's very intuitive of you, Melli. That describes them exactly. Anyway, this isn't getting us anywhere. We're discussing you and Gareth."

I felt like I was being painted into a corner. "Isn't there anybody else? Maybe one of the other girls wants to marry

Gareth…"

"Believe me when I say that I didn't make this decision lightly. India and I looked at all the available girls and you were the best, based on many criteria. The other reason is that he actually likes you, and you appear to like him."

"I did until he began acting weird."

"How?"

"Trying to be my boyfriend—getting angry if I refused."

"But you wouldn't be refusing any more, you see. He will be very happy. Contented. Also, Will has promised to spend more time with Gareth, and is also looking into other ways to lessen the…well…problems."

"Like what?"

"Well, you know that Gareth's work roster has included working with George. Will thinks he might be better suited to the sciences."

"So where will he be?"

"Naturally he won't be returning to the schoolhouse once you two are married. He will spend half his time helping his father with experiments and the other half working on environmental issues with Marie."

"So, Will won't need my help as much?" I felt tears welling.

Meg gave me a long look. "That won't necessarily be the case. Will likes you as an assistant."

What else could I say? I didn't feel as though I was being given a choice. "I still feel like I'm not ready."

"Okay, well here is an idea that just came to me. See what

you think of this: you and Gareth still marry, but I'll provide you with contraception. That way you won't have babies just yet. Maybe a couple of years? How would that be?"

"What if I still didn't feel ready in a couple of years?"

"Hmm. I don't know. But let's cross that bridge when we come to it, eh?" I could feel Meg relaxing slightly. She was happy with how this was going.

"One thing I don't get—"

Meg gave me a tight smile. "Yes?"

"You sound like you're asking my opinion about this— like I have a choice."

The room fell silent. Meg turned and took a few steps away from me and then she turned back around. "No, Melli. Sadly, I cannot offer you a choice. The decision has been made. I just thought I could appeal to your common-sense and gain your co-operation. That would make things easier for all concerned."

"And if I refuse?"

Meg's eyes flashed in anger. "Then you would not be welcome in this community any longer."

"You'd expel me, like you did Grace?"

"I hope that you'll have enough common sense that you won't force me to take any action."

I hated the feeling of being forced against my will. I couldn't let her win without a fight. "I'm going to think this through. I can't give you an answer now. Tell me one thing though."

"What?" Meg's voice was weakening. I was tiring her out.

"If I did agree to co-operate, where would Gareth and I live?"

Meg shrugged. "I hadn't given that any thought, but now you mention it, I guess I'd get George to build you a new cabin."

I gave Meg a weak smile. At least I'd won a couple of concessions. At least I wouldn't have to become a baby-making machine immediately. And Gareth and I would have a brand new cabin of our own.

I pointed at the first white-board, the one with the chart. "You've made a list of elements needed for our survival…"

"Yes, in the early days I'd look at it often, just to check I wasn't missing anything."

I waved her comment away, impatient with her for interrupting me. "Yes, but you've missed something out. Something important."

I saw Meg's eyes turn to the chart and run down the list. "What? What have I missed?"

"Happiness. In order to live well we have to be happy."

Meg raised her arms and then dropped them. "And this is what you kids—the third generation of survivors—don't understand. We are so fortunate to even be alive. Then add in the fact we have all of these things—" She waved at the board. "You kids have no idea of how lucky you are. We elders—we know. I think our children know. It's *you* that doesn't understand. With all of this…you should be happy.

It's not my job to make you so."

"No. It seems that it is your job to make me unhappy."

"It's just the way it is, Melli. It has to happen."

I know my face looked defiant. "I'll let you know." I didn't wait to be dismissed. I raised my chin and walked out of her house.

Will was leaning against the Beast and jumped to attention as soon as he saw me. He opened the passenger door with a flourish. I noticed that he was watching me carefully, trying to gauge my mood. This must have been difficult; given that I didn't know how I felt.

The thought of marrying Gareth still upset me, but I could see the upside of having a new cabin of my own. All that room. I'd have more time to write and space to do it in. I'd have room to move, room to think.

And my sparkly-eyed former friend would turn into my sparkly-eyed husband and we would probably have special sparkly-eyed children. Or would we? Possibly. Only blue-eyed people had bred with the sparkly-eyes up to that stage. I had no idea whether or not my brown eyes and Gareth's special ones would result in our children having special eyes. It was an interesting question. I'd have to ask India.

Will left me alone with my thoughts for a few minutes, before asking about the interview. I told him what happened. He turned and looked at me. "How do you feel about all of that?"

I shrugged. "A bit better. I gave Meg a hard time at least. She insisted that it's going to happen, and I told her I'd think about it. Do you know she threatened to expel me from the community if I didn't do as she said?"

"That would never happen for many reasons. Your parents would go with you—they'd hardly let you go off on your own—so the community would lose your father. That couldn't happen. I wouldn't allow it, anyway."

I smiled at him. "Thanks. Hey, I have an idea about Grace. I reckon I should go for a run. There is a chance she's hiding, waiting to see me alone."

"Yes. Good idea. Where do you want me to drop you?"

"Back at the settlement. I need to get changed."

"Okay, but there's something you should know, before I take you back."

"What?"

"I'm on your side, kiddo. It won't be long before I'm leader. If you do have to marry Gareth, keep delaying motherhood if that's what you want, and I'll make sure you're never forced in to it. Okay?"

I didn't know what to say. My bottom lip began trembling.

"Also, I'll be watching him. He won't be allowed to hurt you. If he ever does, come straight to me, okay? Don't try to hide it. The other thing is that I'm going to make him exercise with me. It will exhaust him until he gets fit. He won't have the energy to be much of a problem to you."

"That's nice to know."

Will looked at me and smiled. "You're one of my favourite people, Melli. I won't let anyone hurt you." We turned into the settlement. "Just find Grace for me, will you?"

I crept into the family cabin. Dad's people-mover wasn't at the settlement, which meant he'd probably gone back to the farm the previous night. Mum would still be around, though, and I didn't feel like seeing her just then. I wanted to find Grace.

I grabbed shorts, socks, shoes, t-shirt and underwear. I had these in my arms and was about to leave the cabin when there was a gentle knock on the door. I cursed and looked out the window. It was Isabella.

"Hey, Melli. It's just me, Bella. I need a quick word."

I opened the door just enough for her to slip through and closed it quickly. The girl looked happier.

"I just wanted to say thanks. You were a good friend through all of that mess. I didn't realise how nice you were."

I smiled and touched her on the arm. "Thanks, but have you heard the latest?"

"Yeah, that's the other reason I came. What do you think about marrying my crazy brother?"

"Not much. I've just had the riot act read to me by Meg. She's insisting."

Bella stepped closer and lowered her voice. "You may

not have to worry. Jack was telling me that Gareth has been talking about leaving, has been for months. Wanted him and Evie to go as well. Start up a new settlement. Somewhere a long way from here."

"What, just the three of them?"

"No, others as well."

I let out a long breath. Wow. That would get me off the hook, but what about the settlement? We needed more people, not less. "Do you think he was serious?"

"Jack thought so. Anyway, I've gotta get back. I just thought I'd pop in and say thanks. You kept my secret and I'm grateful, even if I did end up telling someone."

"You look happier at least."

"Heather made me understand that there was no reason for me to feel so…dirty. I had been so ashamed. She helped me see it from another angle." Bella's smile was infectious. "See you later."

My new friend slipped back through the door. I checked the clothing in my arms and left the cabin quickly. Circling around the back of the buildings, I made my way to the caravan where Grace had stayed. I got changed and then looked out the window. The coast was clear. I opened the door and turned left to go back around the perimeter. There were people out and about, performing various duties, but I managed to avoid being seen.

I was at the top of the hill, just about to run down the driveway, when I saw the people-mover driving up. Dad was at the wheel, Gareth beside him and Valerius in the back. This was such an odd turn of events that I forgot about going for a run, and stared at the vehicle in puzzlement.

Gareth didn't wait for Dad to stop the car, but leapt out while it was still moving. He stumbled, but righted himself. He didn't look at me, but ran to Will who had appeared from his workshop.

"He tried to kill me!" Gareth was panting and pointing toward the vehicle. "That—that weirdo—he tried to murder me!"

Will frowned and made a gesture with his hands that you would use to calm an over-excited horse. "Slow down, Gareth. What are you talking about?"

"That weirdo from the future. He set a trap for me. He tried to kill me."

Dad approached the two. Will turned to him. "Is this true, Trent?"

"I didn't see it—I was here at the time so I'm not sure. I don't know why he would, though."

Will frowned. "Good point. Why do you think he'd want you dead, Gareth?"

"I don't know. He's mad!"

Will walked toward the vehicle and made a sign that he wanted Valerius to join them. The door opened and the man, still in full uniform, stood and began hobbling toward the group.

"What happened to you?" said Will.

Gareth didn't give Valerius a chance to reply. "That happened when he tried to kill me."

A group of interested onlookers was starting to gather. Will looked around and sighed. "Okay, everyone. Go about your business, please. Trent, Gareth and Valerius, come into my workshop." He saw me. "You too, Melli. This is your business now."

Gareth spun around and looked at me. "Why? Why are you including her?"

"You know why, Gareth. She's about to become your wife."

Gareth stopped and folded his arms. "No. No way. I've already told Trent here. I'm not marrying her. If you try to make me, I'll run away."

Will frowned. "I thought you'd be happy with that idea— thought you liked Melli. So why not?"

Gareth snorted. "You wouldn't expect me to actually marry one of the dumb brown-eyes, would you?"

EXTREME ACTION

Although the warm weather had begun, the early mornings were still deliciously cool. I hit the road early, marvelling at my body and how it responded to my need to run. It felt glorious.

I had been denied my planned search for Grace the previous afternoon. Gareth's extraordinary announcement had set the cat among the pigeons. Meg was fetched. William became involved. It went on for hours. In the end, Gareth still remained resolute. I had to admire his bravery—against all opposition he flatly refused to marry me and threatened to leave the settlement if forced. "I never said I wanted to marry her. I just hoped she'd—you know—be my girlfriend if you know what I mean. I just wanted…you know…"

Meg sighed. "Yes, we get the picture. Nonetheless, it is the best option, Gareth. You clearly have problems—"

Will interrupted. "Okay, well this is what I reckon. Gareth is my son and I believe I've been neglectful of my duties as a father. Leena wanted to raise him on her own, but that hasn't been good for the boy. He needs a masculine influence. That starts now. Today will be a new start."

Meg frowned. "That's all well and good, Will, but what about what happened to Bella? What about the girls in this settlement?"

Will looked at Gareth. "There will be no more of that. I guarantee it. Gareth, Jack and I will go on a short holiday to the beach. When we return, things will be different."

Gareth leaned against the door-frame. "What about Valerius? Nobody's saying anything about how he tried to kill me."

Will nodded. "I'll look into that when we get back from our holiday."

Now, as I ran, I could laugh at these turns of events. The past couple of days had been an emotional roller-coaster, but for now I was free. No marriage, no Gareth, and unless I was mistaken, I'd just found Grace.

I had seen a flash of white among the untidy trees in the park where we'd sat and talked once. I slowed and looked again. Yes, there was my friend and both of her eyes were free of bandages. I looked around to make sure there wasn't anybody following me.

"I found you at last!"

Grace came forward with a big smile and hugged me. It felt good. "Yes, you didn't think I'd go away without saying goodbye, surely?"

"No. Of course not. But you're not leaving the area, are you?"

"Not until I sort out a few things. Tell me what's been going on."

I told her about the extraordinary events of the past few days. Grace was smiling. I looked into her left, damaged eye. It had healed, but the colour of the iris was weird. It was like a special sparkly-eye in colour, with the blues, greens and violets, but dull, almost milky.

"And," I said laughing, "Gareth reckons Valerius tried to kill him."

"I see." Grace didn't seem surprised.

"I figured that he made it up, that he was just seeking attention."

"Perhaps. Did anybody believe Gareth?"

"No. Not really."

"And Gareth has been threatening to leave. We can't have that."

"Yes, and Bella said he's been talking about leaving for some time, to start a new settlement. Has asked Jack and Evie to go too."

"We absolutely must act before Gareth leaves."

"You think he's serious then, about going?"

"Yes. Maybe not immediately, but it will happen. I think it's time that Valerius and I joined forces." Grace stopped and thought for a moment. "How do you think Valerius and I could meet up?"

"Name a time and place. I'll get him there."

"Good girl. We'll need to include you in on our plans, I think."

"I'll do what I can. Hey, there's something else you should know."

"What?"

"It's Will. He tried to find you. He's a bit lost, I think. Misses you."

I noticed how Grace's face changed. It became soft, and a gentle smile hovered around her lips. I'd seen this look on some of the girls in the community, just before they succumbed to marriage and breeding. Love-struck. Grace shook her head as if to clear it. "That's a thought for another time, if ever. No. Never. For now, we have to concentrate hard and fix the Gareth problem. If you're going to help us, you'll need to know the whole story."

"You're going to tell me at last?"

"I believe I can trust you, Melli. Is that right?"

"Of course. I think I've figured most of it out anyway."

"You're a smart girl, so of course you have. The thing is that you may not agree with what I have to do. What if you found my plans unpalatable? What if you didn't agree with them?"

"I doubt—"

"No. I mean it, Melli. Valerius and I will be talking about extreme action. Can you give me your word that if you don't agree with it, you won't say anything to anyone else in the community?"

"Yes, I guess so."

"I'm sorry, Melli, but that isn't good enough. Do I have your solemn vow?"

I laughed. So serious. "Yes. You have my solemn vow."

Grace searched my face and then nodded. "Alright. First things first. There is a small house not far from here where I'll camp for a couple of days. I'll take you there now, so you can lead Valerius to it later. I'll discuss plans with him, then we'll tell you all about it."

"Fine."

"And you'll have to make him understand that he is to move to this place, not just visit. He is to leave the settlement. He's to bring all weapons. He is also to bring the device that enables returning to our time. He's to leave nothing at the settlement. Okay?"

"Okay! Understood."

"And remember he knows me as Aelia." Grace turned and waved at me to follow her. There was no conversation, just a hard slog through overgrown vegetation. She led me to a house that wasn't habitable as far as I was concerned. When I said so, Grace shrugged. "It has a roof, plus a natural spring just nearby. I won't be here long. My work is almost finished."

"What about food. Should I bring you some?"

"If you can without raising questions, that would be welcome. Otherwise don't worry. Water is the main thing. I can go hungry."

I admired this woman so much. There was a sureness to everything she did. A certainty that what she did was right. A grim determination to succeed, whatever the obstacles. She was incredible.

As I ran back to the community, I began wondering just how extreme this 'extreme action' was going to be.

Valerius was a weird guy. I mean really weird. Trying to give him the important message from Grace proved difficult. At first he didn't want to talk to me at all and then he didn't trust what I was saying. After that, it was a problem to get him to agree, mainly because he'd damaged his ankle at the farm and didn't want to walk to the house where Grace was staying. Valerius didn't handle personal discomfort well.

Finally, I had him convinced that this had to happen or he'd be letting Aelia down. We were to leave the settlement in the cover of darkness at nine o'clock that night. Valerius was to be ready and packed. He was to bring weapons and the device which allowed him to return to the future.

Will, Gareth and Jack were busy making plans for their

break away from the settlement. I could see the three of them, talking noisily and placing items in a pile ready to pack. They would leave the next day.

I could tell that Gareth knew I was there, watching, but he wouldn't look at me. Was he embarrassed about recent events, or just finished with me as a friend? Either way it was okay by me. I was disturbed by how he had treated me and what he'd said. I no longer trusted or liked him. The thought of what he'd tried to do with Bella made my stomach lurch. I didn't want to be his friend any more.

Will was the reason I stood and watched the goings on of the three of them. His face had changed since Grace was expelled, in a way I couldn't quite put my finger on. He looked older, like there was suffering going on deep inside him. He had aged. He noticed me and jogged over. "Any news?" he said, searching my face for clues.

I hated lying to him but had no choice. "No, I can't find her. I'll try again tonight."

Will's shoulders sagged and he returned to the packing with a heavy step.

I went to my family's cabin to seek out my mother. We hadn't spoken since the night Dad had told me I was to be married to Gareth. I knew Mum had been on my side and had fought for my rights. I was keen to let her know I was alright. She was glad to see me. We hugged and chatted. It felt good.

I told her that the friction between her and Dad over me

had made me sad. I asked that she not hold anything against Dad now. Everything had turned out alright. I explained to her that Dad had to deal with Meg often and that she always made him obey her. "You don't have much to do with Meg. You don't know what it's like. She just doesn't take no for an answer. I won't stay angry with him, so you shouldn't. It was being done to me, after all."

Mum smiled sadly and nodded. I was sure she wasn't happy while she and Dad weren't close. I kissed her on the cheek and left her to her thoughts.

That afternoon I helped Heather in the schoolhouse, finding the little children a balm for the things that weighed heavily on my mind. I knew I was taking a risk, helping Grace, but nothing else made sense to me at that time. I was nervous, but having the little kids look at me with that special, unconditional love that only small children can show, made me feel better.

I went on my run as usual in the evening, mostly to appear normal. Will would be watching, hoping I'd come back with good news. I turned left as I exited the driveway, going in the opposite direction to Grace's house. I sprinted for a while, which felt brilliant, then steadied into a well-paced jog.

When I arrived back, I shook my head at an anxious looking Will and then went to get food. I'd need plenty of energy for the events of the evening.

Valerius was being tiresome, and I was worried about reaching the house at the time when Grace said we should. She had been very specific. "Be there at exactly nine-thirty," she'd said, watching my face to make sure I understood. "If you're going to arrive early, slow down but don't be late. This is important."

"Why?"

"Because of what I have planned. Don't worry about that now."

It was easy for her to say, but hard for me to follow. Valerius was moaning and hanging back. I'd had to take his bag and hang it over my shoulder. Next, I had to find him a stick to support his damaged ankle. Sometimes he had to lean on me. Fortunately, he wasn't a heavy man.

I tried to take his mind off the injury by making conversation. "Tell me about time travel, Valerius."

I felt the man shrug in the darkness. "Long, boring, uncomfortable."

"How come you have a device for returning to your time but Aelia doesn't?"

"Anything with metal has to be sent separately, after humans are transferred. It wasn't done with Aelia because of the circumstances of her leaving."

"Which were?"

"William and Martin were escaping. Aelia was trying to stop them. The portal was closing. The Emperor and I were after the men. Aelia got caught up in it all and was transported by mistake."

"Yes, she told me that."

"The Emperor, Titus XI, threw a tantrum. He's an unstable man."

"Did you say Titus? That's funny."

"Why?"

"That's who Gareth was talking about. In ancient Rome. Emperor Titus. He admired him and wanted to be just like him."

"Really?"

"He even spoke about changing his name. To Titus, that is."

Valerius went silent for a moment. "Then I was right. That has just confirmed it."

"What do you mean?"

"We must deal with Gareth as a matter of urgency. I'm glad we're on our way to Aelia. I will devise a plan and then issue her with orders. She will have to deal with him."

Valerius and I approached the house wearily. My companion had been quiet for much of the later part of the walk, as though he were using every last brain cell to work on the problem of Gareth. Or maybe he was just tired and in pain. We trudged through the darkness, arriving at the house a minute or two later than Grace had requested.

A high-pitched scream rang through the night, scaring the

hell out of me. It was so loud! I felt Valerius jump in alarm. A second scream came soon after the first. I ran to the house, with Valerius hobbling behind me. We crashed through what was left of the door, and I saw a scene that made me gasp.

The room was dimly lit, with just one lamp. Gareth was there and he had hold of Grace. He was standing behind her, and had his arm around her neck. Grotesque shadows were dancing on the walls and ceiling.

With his free hand, Gareth had hold of Grace's blouse and was trying to rip it open. He was grunting and muttering. He seemed weird—like in a trance. Grace was red-faced and making whimpering noises. Both she and Gareth seemed oblivious to our presence.

I moved to run towards Grace and help her, but Valerius grabbed my arm. "Wait," he said in a low tone. He took his bag from me and placed it on the floor. Next he knelt down and rummaged through the contents.

I was distressed at the scene before me and was considering ignoring Valerius' instructions. Someone had to help Grace. She looked like she was choking. I began to move forward again, but Valerius dragged me back. He rummaged in the bag some more and then grunted in satisfaction. He produced a strange, disk like object from the bag. He turned it on its side and checked some settings.

We had only been in the house for a matter of seconds, but it seemed like hours. It was as though time had slowed down to a trickle. I had once seen an hourglass in the cupboard of the original house. I'd been in awe of how slowly the sand trickled from one bulb to the other. This flashed into my mind while this scene was unfolding. The sand was now moving just one grain at a time. Everything was in the slowest motion.

Grace became aware of us. When she saw the device Valerius was holding, her eyes widened. Then she seemed to find some extra energy. She performed a manoeuvre that freed her from Gareth's hold, and then pushed him away from her. Valerius aimed the device and fired. What happened next was the stuff of nightmares.

A beam of light of the brightest blue flashed across the distance between the weapon and Gareth. It was so bright it made me blink. When my eyes re-opened I found that Gareth had disappeared. All that was left was a mound of what looked like ash. I cried out in shock.

Then there was another extraordinary event, stranger than the first. I felt a pop of energy from beside me. It was like some air had been sucked away from where Valerius stood. When I turned around, it was to find an empty space where Valerius had been. All that remained were his clothes, boots, hat and weapon. He had vanished in the matter of a second. I stood, looking dumbly at the space where he had been. I was aware that my mouth was hanging open.

Grace was brushing herself down and straightening her clothing. She smiled at me. "That went well," she said.

It was a few seconds before I found my voice. "It did?

But Gareth, he's dead?"

"Yes. That was necessary, unfortunately."

"But—"

"Brilliant. Well done. Listen, I'll explain all this later, but I need you to do one more thing tonight. Is that alright? Sorry, you must be tired."

"But—Gareth's dead. I don't get it."

"Melli. I know it's hard. I realise it's a shock. If you can't help me, just say so."

My mind had gone blank. I felt tremors running through my body. Gareth was dead, just like that.

Grace came and put her hands on my shoulders. She looked into my face. "Listen to me. It's all nearly done. I just need one more thing, but you can say no."

"You don't understand, Grace. Listen to me. I don't know what it's like in your time, but it's different here. We don't kill people. We just don't. It can't happen."

Grace was still looking into my face. When she began talking again, the words came slower than normal. "Well it did happen, Melli. And now it can't be undone. Understand?"

"This was the extreme action you were talking about? That's why you wouldn't tell me your plans! You knew that I'd never even consider this as a solution, because the concept of taking a life just doesn't exist. The very thought is absurd."

"Yes, Melli. That's why I couldn't tell you. In the future, in my time, the Emperor executed my father. Then he burned our house down with my mother inside. I thought my brother and sister had been burned to death as well, but later discovered the Emperor had kept them. He was using them as sexual playthings for himself and his guards." Grace took a shuddering breath. "This wasn't an isolated case—he did this to many families—all brown-eyes of course. Never Elite. Taking Gareth's life may have saved my parents, my siblings, my love. It may have saved countless other people. My world may now be a peaceful and happy place."

I gave my whole body a shake. I had to control myself. Grace and I were warrior sisters.

"What do you need?" I said. I noticed how flat my voice had gone. It was like something had been extinguished inside of me.

"You saw what happened here. You're my witness. I didn't kill Gareth, right? I didn't kill the son of Will, and grandson of Meg, William and India, did I?"

"No. I saw Valerius do it."

"That's right, but I want to explain this to Will. He needs to know the whole story from me. Can you send him to me? Tonight? Now?"

I thought about the walk back to the settlement in the dark. Then I had to return again with Will. Then, later, the walk back again. I wasn't sure I had enough energy left. Not after what I'd just seen. It was as though Grace read my thoughts. "No need for you to come back with him."

"How will he know where to come?"

Grace motioned with one hand. "Pass me Valerius' bag." She rummaged inside for a moment. She found a device that made her smile, and she slipped this in a pocket. She rummaged some more and pulled out a small screen. She pressed buttons and a red dot appeared. "Give this to Will. Tell him it will lead him to me. Tell him to come in secret. Okay?"

"Sure. Then, what will happen after that. What will you do?"

"Come back tomorrow and we'll discuss that. But go now, quickly. Would you?"

"Sure. After you tell me one more thing."

"What?"

"Where did Valerius go?"

Grace smiled. "Valerius was a direct descendant of Gareth, you see. When the boy was neutralised, Valerius simply no longer existed. Never did, really."

I frowned. "But wouldn't he have realised that?"

"No, Valerius always thought he was smarter than what he actually was. Sometimes he was just plain stupid. Imagine thinking he could use the Pigeon device to send messages to the Commander." Grace laughed. "How could he when the Commander won't be born for several hundred years yet."

I frowned. "Gosh—"

"Go now, sweetheart." She kissed me on the cheek. "Thank you so much. Between you and me, we just saved the world. Go quickly now."

I did what she asked. I moved as fast as I could, often tripping on tree roots or getting tangled in lantana. It seemed a long way back to the settlement alone and in the dark. But I did it. I did it for Grace.

I found Will in his cabin, sitting with Ruth, Jack, Evie and Bella. It was a nice domestic scene; Ruth was sewing while Will scribbled in his notebook. I could hear the younger children asleep in another room, their heavy breathing and shuffling sounding clear on the quiet night.

Jack and Bella were talking in a corner, while Evie was reading a book. It seemed a shame to disturb this peaceful family.

I adjusted my position on the veranda until only Will was in sight. I waved my arms around until he looked up, frowning. As soon as he realised who was trying to gain his attention, he nodded.

I saw him place the notebook and pen back in his shirt pocket, before standing and stretching. He said something to Ruth and she nodded. I moved from the veranda to a place in the shadows of the big fig tree.

Will loped over to stand with me. His face was lit with excitement. "You've found her?"

I thought about his son and felt sad. It was right that Grace break the news to him. "Yeah. She asked if you'd go and see her."

"Great. I'll go straight away. Where is she?"

I handed him the device with the red dot. "She said this would lead you there. She's in a house not far from here, but it's fairly rough going through the vegetation."

Will nodded, smiling. "Wonderful." He began walking and then stopped and turned. "You aren't coming?"

"No, I'm exhausted. It's time I hit the sack."

Will came back and cupped my cheek with his hand. "Yes, you look tired. Actually, you look shattered. Are you okay?"

I nodded. "I'll be good after a rest. Go now. She's waiting."

Will leaned over and kissed me on the forehead, an act of friendship rather than passion, but it felt nice all the same. "Thanks, Melli."

I smiled weakly as Will began walking down the driveway. I watched his progress until the white of his shirt blended into the darkness. I stood for several minutes after that, looking into an empty space.

I didn't want to go to the family cabin, where I would be asked questions I couldn't answer. I felt as though I was suffering some sort of minor shock from the night's events—my whole body was shaking.

I remembered the empty caravan where Grace had stayed, and headed there. Solitude was what I craved more than anything.

My dreams that night were violent and distressing. They kept waking me. Gareth died before my eyes over and over again, and I would wake, gasping for breath each time it happened.

Grace and I, the warrior sisters, may have saved the world, but I was confused and upset. I hoped it was worth it.

DISAPPEARANCES

I woke next morning to cries of alarm. Ruth was running around the settlement calling out for Will. Jack and Evie were banging on doors, asking questions of the occupants. Nobody came to the caravan—they thought it was empty.

I could hear various conversations. Valerius wasn't in the shed. Gareth hadn't been seen by Leena since the night before. Will had gone for a walk late in the evening and hadn't returned. My name was mentioned. When was I last seen?

It was widely known that Grace had been expelled. Where was she? William had moved back to Meg's when Valerius came back from the farm, so he was okay.

I was tired and my body was aching from the previous

day's exertions. My head was pounding. I roused myself, however, and dressed quickly. One question kept running through my mind. Why hadn't Will returned?

I stood at the window of the caravan and waited until I couldn't see anyone. The voices had faded into the distance. I opened the caravan door carefully and slipped out.

By now I knew how to skirt around the settlement and leave without being noticed. One of the dogs barked playfully, but was fortunately ignored.

One thing was for certain—I was thoroughly sick of fighting my way through the vegetation that surrounded the house where Grace was hiding. I plunged into it with ill humour, deciding this would be the last time I did it. If Grace wanted to see me again, she'd have to come to me.

Finally, I arrived. I stood at the edge of the clearing and considered the house. It looked quiet. If Grace was inside, and Will was still with her, maybe they'd be busy with each other. I might be disturbing them. Bad luck, I thought. I wasn't in a mood to worry about such things. I was really pissed off. Grace had told me to come and I had. I would hear what she had to say, tell Will that everyone was worried about him and then leave.

I began calling out, "Grace! Will!" but nobody answered. I knocked on the ruin of a door. After a few seconds, I entered.

The house echoed in a way that suggested it was empty. Where were they? I looked around and found clues. Beside

Gareth's pile of ash sat Valerius' bag with all the contents intact, even the device that Grace handed to me the night before—the one that she set so that Will would find her. This proved that Will had arrived as planned.

I saw a piece of paper that hadn't been there the night before. It had been ripped from Will's special notebook and was written in his handwriting. It said, '*Grace wants you to write about what happened. Meg's account won't be accurate. The people of the future need to know about the events of the past few weeks. It is important. Will. xxx*'

I placed this note in my pocket with sadness. I'd already begun to understand that I wouldn't see either of my favourite people again. Had they run away together?

Outside I found something else. It was a patch of long grass that had been flattened. Sitting in this area were several items. There were Will's belt and pocket knife. A device, the same one that I saw Grace place in her pocket the night before, also lay there. I was certain it was the object needed to trigger transportation through time to the future.

I sat on this patch of grass for ages, deep in thought. Later, I came to, realising I had dozed off. The exertions and high emotions of the day before had taken their toll. I woke with a mind full of thoughts, all the events and ideas tumbling around in my head. I needed to put them in some sort of order.

This is what I now knew to be true:

The mad Emperor who caused all the grief in Grace's

time was Titus XI. Gareth was Titus I. I had sort of realised this earlier but didn't know that Grace's mission, her reason for travelling back in time, had always been to 'neutralise' Gareth. Valerius had been late to put all the pieces together but had finally reached the correct conclusion. He too wanted the boy dead.

Grace had somehow arranged for Gareth to be there at nine-thirty, so that Valerius would kill him. Why had she thought this necessary? It must have been difficult to arrange. The answer was that she didn't want his blood on her hands. Did she plan for Gareth to be attacking her at the time? That could have been accidental, although I'm sure she was strong enough to repel an attack from him. She had, after all, been trained in combat and self-defence techniques. When Valerius and I came on the scene, she didn't seem to be trying hard enough to get away, not until it was necessary to do so.

And Grace had taken Will with her, back to the time where she belonged. Why had she done that? It was so out of character that I couldn't even process the idea properly. If anyone had told me they thought there was a chance of this, I would have laughed at them. It didn't make sense. She had removed a person from the community who was vital to its well-being, an act which could be detrimental to the future. Why? Why would she do something like that?

I thought harder about this. She would not have planned it that way. Surely not. Maybe it was a sudden decision. Did

Will talk her into it? Maybe love was just too strong. Clearly I had missed something there—they must have spent more time together than I knew. They had hidden this from me.

What would life be like back in her time when she arrived there? Had she really improved things? Maybe her boyfriend, Caelius, was still alive, seeing as Valerius' brother probably didn't exist. How would that work with Will turning up as well? I felt my head starting to throb. All this time travel stuff was confusing.

I looked at the device that was still clutched in my hand, the one that triggered time travel. I opened the lid and inspected the settings. The biggest button on this device was green and it had a ring of flashing lights around it. I guessed that would be the one you would press when you were ready to be transported.

I considered this green button for the longest time. Eventually, I closed the lid sadly, and placed the object in a pocket of my overalls, the one that buttoned down tightly.

I began walking back to the settlement with legs that felt like lead. I barely noticed the tangles of vegetation. Too many questions were running through my mind.

Who would I tell about this? Did I need to tell anybody? Would anyone want to know the truth?

I came to the conclusion that Meg had to be told. Not only was she the leader, but she had the right to know that her grandson had died. She also needed to know what had happened to her son.

How in the hell would I explain all this to her? I was only thirteen for heaven's sakes.

I turned in the direction of Meg's house with a heavy heart.

FLYING

Three years later I took my first solo flight.

Grace, when she first learned that my greatest wish was to fly, had spoken to William and Will. Both of these men became excited at the prospect of building an aircraft and did some preliminary work on the plans. After Will disappeared, his father continued working on the project, bringing Jack, Evie and Isabella in to help. I think it was a good thing for them to work on at the time, to distract them from the bad events that had just happened.

William included me in the aviation lessons that his grandchildren took. They all had to learn about flight in order to properly construct the aircraft. I had to learn about it to become a pilot.

The whole project was complex and time consuming. Some of the parts were difficult to obtain. The world outside our two settlements was a ruin, so scavenging forays were problematic. Every small detail of the project caused problems and we needed to adapt our thinking for flexible solutions.

When it was nearly time for the first test-flight, a take-off/landing strip needed to be organised. It was decided that the road between the settlement and Meg's house would be ideal, as long as we lopped off some overhanging branches of the trees that bordered it. We needed to repair sections of the road and this was achieved quickly by Luke and his boys.

How can I describe that first flight? Oh, it was glorious! It took place on a clear, blue-skied day when fluffy clouds drifted on the horizon, hanging over the sea.

At first I circled around Maleny until I became confident about the aircraft and my ability to handle it. Then I banked and followed roads to Nambour, so that I could buzz the workers on The Farm. My father ran out of a building, waving his hat and hooting.

After that, I headed east to the coast. At first I skirted along the shoreline, looking at the ruined remains of high-rise buildings. It looked strange from the air. I could see how Mother Nature had reclaimed her hold on Earth.

I turned to the left and dropped altitude, flying low over the rolling waves. By this time, the little aircraft had become an extension of me. We had bonded. I felt safe in its embrace. I didn't want to return home.

I figured this was Grace's gift to me, a thank you for my help and loyalty. Or did she know that she'd eventually have to leave me behind without explanation, and this was her apology?

Knowing that William and the others would be worried, I turned and began heading west toward the settlement. Before I reached land, I took the time travel device out of my pocket and dropped it into the sea. In that way I made sure that I'd never be tempted to press the buttons that could send me forward in time and be reunited with my two favourite people. Enough harm had been caused by time travellers being transported. I wanted to see an end to it. I hoped that Grace, back in her own time, made sure that nobody else travelled back to Maleny ever again.

As I approached the small cluster of buildings that housed all that was left of mankind, I had a sort of epiphany. I knew then that we'd all be okay, that we would survive and thrive even without the talented Will, because if we could build an aircraft and fly like the birds, then we could do anything. We were awesome. We just had to remember that. We had to stretch and challenge ourselves daily.

As I banked around to line up the road for my first ever landing, it was with a confident and relaxed smile.

We would all be fine.

SAVING GRACE

What finally prompted me to record these happenings was Meg's passing.

The disappearance of Will and the death of Gareth had knocked the stuffing out of our leader. She suffered a sort of breakdown and was weak for a long time. William stayed at her house to help, but it was my company she wanted. I would spend an hour or two with her on most days in the years until she died. In this way, I came to fully appreciate the special person she was, and learned a lot from her.

She and I only ever argued once. It was early on, a few months after those terrible events. Meg suggested that Grace had played me for a sucker, that she'd manipulated me into helping her. She went on to say that I had been a pawn in Grace's game, albeit an innocent one.

This angered me. I was strong in my denial, telling her that I had helped Grace willingly because I liked and admired her. The argument was over quickly, both of us deciding that those events were in the past and we should agree to differ.

Now, with the benefit of hindsight, I can see that Meg had a point. Maybe I was gullible back then. Maybe I was drawn into Grace's plans after falling under her spell. I can easily forgive myself, however. I had only been thirteen at the time. I had also been sheltered from the worst that humanity had to offer, unlike Grace who had seen it all. In any case, it was in the past and nothing could change it now.

As Meg weakened and lost the ability to lead, there were discussions about what would happen next. Will's absence left a gaping hole. Old William wasn't a natural leader, nor was he interested in becoming one. My two grandfathers, Luke and George, lacked leadership skills. Heather was able to inspire children, but not adults. India had never been a people person, her only friend being Meg.

I think it was because I had seen the future through Grace's eyes that I was able to see the present with more clarity. I saw what needed to be done in the settlement better than Meg did. People's attitudes toward me began changing. I was invited to sit at the elders' table for dinner where I would be consulted on issues both large and small. As I walked around the settlement, I was asked for advice on all sorts of matters. I began to spend more and more time on issues to do with the well-being of our community.

I discovered I had a knack for seeing a problem clearly and then being able to bring together the right team of people to solve it. Those people did what I asked them to do with a good attitude. In this manner, without trying, or indeed wanting to, I became the leader of the community in my nineteenth year.

I do things differently to the way Meg operated. I don't demand co-operation, but somehow just achieve it. Instead of having the emphasis on repopulating the world, I have shifted focus to the health and wellbeing of the women in the community.

I have made another change: anyone with natural gifts in the arts had been largely ignored under Meg's leadership. I have fostered the talents of musicians, artists and writers, making sure they have the time and tools to develop their special gifts. This has enriched the community, and I consider it my greatest achievement so far.

We put these talents to good use just prior to Meg's death when we held a memorial service for Gareth. This was held on the tenth anniversary of his death. Clementine, a singer and songwriter, and her twin Charlie, a composer and musician, created a piece they called 'Song for Gareth'. This was the first real piece of music composed and performed for the community as a whole and it was quite wonderful.

This music was also performed on a clear, summer

morning a few weeks later as Meg's body was lowered into the soil which lay under the old fig tree. Clementine's clear voice was accompanied by the strange 'whoop-whoop' call of the Pheasant Coucal which nested in the forest. There were few dry eyes that morning.

Subsequently, 'Song for Gareth' had its name changed to 'Requiem for Gareth' and then 'Requiem for Titus'. It will be performed during any formal ceremonies held in the community in the future.

On a sad note, I am beginning to despair about the human capacity for violence. It has crept into our community like a thief in the night, affecting the third and fourth generations of survivors. Is violence an innate quality of the human race? This thought keeps me awake at night. So far there have been just minor skirmishes, teenage boys forming into small groups and agitating until there is a fight. We have come down hard on these boys and tried to teach them the benefits of a peaceful society, but I can still feel the menace which shimmers malevolently just below the surface of our calm settlement.

Then, there have been aspects of my personal life that needed careful thought. My decision to delay becoming a mother had developed into something deeper. I wondered if it would be best if I didn't wed and bear children at all. I could see that my new role as leader would be all-encompassing, would take more hours in a day than I had time for. How could I also have a family? I recalled a quote I'd seen once which summed up my feelings exactly. It was, by the Tudor Queen Elizabeth I: '*Better beggar woman and single than Queen and married.*' It made me smile.

Not long after that, however, I had a shocking thought. If Grace *was* a direct descendant of mine, and the time for becoming pregnant with the child that would carry on my line to her passed, would Grace simply disappear like Valerius? How scary was that? It would be like murdering her.

I hurried to William and asked his opinion. He nodded slowly and considered his answer carefully. "That's a big question, dear girl. I wish I had a definite answer for you."

I became impatient. "Is there even a chance of that? A chance that she could be going about her life in the future and disappear? Just because I didn't have the children I would have had otherwise?"

"A chance? Maybe an outside one. You're not even sure she was a descendant of yours."

"She thought she might be."

"Yes, there were a great many similarities between you two."

"So there could be a chance? She and Will could be somewhere, enjoying themselves. Maybe they've had their own children. They could be in a field, having a picnic in the sunshine with their little family. There could be a pop of energy, a sucking of air, and Grace would be gone, just like that." I clicked my fingers for emphasis. "So would the children. Will would be left there all alone and not know why.

How terrible would that be?"

"Yes, that is a terrible thought indeed."

"What do you think I should do?"

"You're a smart girl, Melli. You will work it out."

These thoughts would not leave me alone. Even if it was just an outside chance, the cost of getting it wrong was too high. I couldn't live with that.

I spoke to India and Ruth. We devised a plan in which I could become pregnant by a process involving fertilising my egg in India's laboratory and then planting the embryo inside me. In that way we could ensure I had only one child and we could select the best father based on genetic factors. The father was Jack, Will and Ruth's son. It would be the first time a member of the Luke and Connie/George and Heather side bred with anybody from the Meg and William/India camp. As I write this, the baby moves inside me. It fills me with a joy I cannot adequately express.

I hope that creating this special new person will mean I am saving Grace. Or at least ensuring she still exists. I don't know if this is the case, but can only wish it with all my might.

With Meg's passing, plans were made to put her diaries somewhere safe. George volunteered to make a container to place them in, one which would protect them from harm. He also insisted that each volume be individually wrapped and that damp protection materials were placed with them.

Luke has found a site to position the diaries, outside the

ruins of the Maleny library. The men will dig a hole, line it with concrete and then place the container inside that. They will create a plaque to lay on top, giving information about what lays beneath.

As we were making these plans, I realised this was the time to write this story so that my record could be placed with Meg's. Grace was right, Meg's account of what happened when the time travellers returned wasn't accurate. It missed vital details. My story is necessary to keep the facts straight.

Grace once asked me about my notebook and what I wrote in it. I told her about my stories and invited her to read one. She looked at the pages and handed the book back to me, explaining that people couldn't read handwriting in the time where she belonged. That worries me now. Will people in the future be able to read Meg's diaries? I've taken the precaution of typing this story into one of Will's computers and printing it on the precious reserves of paper we have stored. Hopefully this will overcome the problem, for this book at least.

My greatest wish is that Grace and Will eventually get to read it.

Melisandre

Maleny 2059

<<<<>>>>

AUTHOR'S NOTE

The characters from Maleny and beyond have been with me for many years now. They have filled my dreams and invaded my waking thoughts for all that time. I have found them to be good company.

They were a writer's dream come true, walking onto stage and saying their lines with little prompting. Sometimes they surprised me with sudden plot changes, or behaviour that I hadn't seen coming. This never failed to delight me.

Meg, Grace and Melisandre have been great heroes, each with their distinctive methods of achieving their goals. They were all kick-arse gals who displayed great inner strength.

I admired Derek a great deal, and felt a sense of loss when he decided to return to his family. At least his line continued in Ruth and Leena's descendants.

Luke and Connie's story was touching. They had an enduring and loving relationship which spanned many decades. Luke remained loyal to Connie, despite her serious health problems. He was one of the good guys.

I would like to thank my readers for coming on this journey with me. Your support, whether it be liking my Brenda Cheers Author Facebook page, posting reviews on Amazon/Goodreads, or just getting in touch to ask questions (when is the next in the series being published?) has been appreciated. It has driven me back to the writing desk on days when it would have been easier to do something else. Bless you.

These books would not have been possible without the efforts of people close to me. I have two trusted readers of the early drafts whose advice I rely on heavily. Thank you Tez and Bex.

Tracey and Laura swoop in during the late stages of manuscript development. By that stage I am blind to minor errors and rely heavily on their advice. Many thanks.

My writing goes on, despite the Strange Worlds story coming to a close. I would be delighted if you'd stay on this journey with me.

Brenda Cheers

ABOUT THE AUTHOR

Brenda is a novelist and short story writer from Brisbane, Australia. 'Requiem for Titus' is her eighth published novel.

Also by Brenda Cheers

www.ingramcontent.com/pod-product-compliance
Lightning Source LLC
Chambersburg PA
CBHW050400030726
47503CB00006B/1946